The Perfect Mile

By
Ken Knipple

Books written by Ken Knipple

Green Eyes	Wildcards
Saigon Tea	Seeds In The Wind
An Angel's Prayer	Paid In Full
The Waitress	Page Two
Three From The Sea	Garden In The Sun
The Salesman	It Happens
Look Jane, See Dick	Tsunami
Sandcastle	A Merritt To All
Our Id	The Perfect Mile
And In This Corner	Princess
A Small World	Pops
A View From The Cheap Seats	Chance's
The Survivor	Shoot The Moon
A Sea Story	A Spark Of Reason
A Beautiful Sight	One In A Million
Toni	The Atlantis

Money Isn't Everything (But It Helps)
Anna's World

The Price War's Series: by Ken Knipple
- Awakening Price
- Bachelor Girl
- Charging Full Price
- The Price You Pay

Amazingly, since first starting this novel, it has been announced by several automotive manufactures, such as Audi, Mercedes, Uber and GM, that they are in fact tested autonomous vehicles on the open roads. That means that the technology that is mentioned in this book exist today. It is technology that will most likely be put into use at some time in the near future. Soon all vehicles will have autopilots in them, just like aircraft do and just like the vehicles that were developed in this book does.

Chapter One

The huge executive chair made no noise on the plush carpet as Eloise, or Elli as she liked to be called, pushed herself away from the desk with her spiked high-heeled shoe, she had it planted firmly on the middle drawer of the huge desk. As she did this, her light-gray skirt slipped upwards, displaying a pair of lovely, long, nylon clad legs and a cream-colored half-slip that she wore under the skirt. Spinning the chair around to face the window of the office, an office that was on the twenty-second floor, the top floor, of the Piedmont Building, she moved her feet to the window sill, spread them in a suggestive manner and then rubbed her hands over the warm, raised, mound that was hidden beneath the smooth black silk of her panties.

"Now the world comes to me, -- and for a change it has to make me happy. Now it's my turn to make and break these unimaginative fucks at my whims and they're going to have to cater to me for a change." She looked down at the junction of her legs and continued speaking. "Take a good look at what I'm showing you, world; because this is the last time you're going to see this unless it's on my terms, on my time and it will be at my pleasure, not yours. It's my turn to pull the strings and watch all those cocks in the business world jump to satisfy my whims."

She slipped her shoes off, sat them on the wide window sill out of the way, then got out of the chair and crawled up onto the sill. Holding her hands on either side of the window to steady herself, she pushed her breast against the window, then she pulled her skirt and slip up and over her naturally flaring hips, she pulled the clothes up to her tiny, trim waist. "This is it, you fuckers, you've all had your shots at me and I'm sorry to have to say that there was not a real man found among any of you cocksucker's."

Being careful not to fall off her precarious perch in the window, she turned around and pulled her panties down. Then grabbing the back of the huge executive office chair to steady herself, she bent over and stuck those beautiful twin globes of her tush against the glass panes. "And this is what you've got to kiss and eat what comes out of it, but only when I'm ready to let you."

She pulled her panties up, then got down from the window, again without falling and straighten her clothes out before setting back down on her chair. A drink would have been nice right about now, but she was high on power and didn't need it right then, that's because the words that the moderator had spoken a short while ago were still echoing in her ears.

"Gentlemen, the stockholder's votes are in and they have elected Miss Masterson as the CEO of Franklin International. Miss Masterson also takes over as Chairman of the Board of Trusties of the Franklin Trust, it's the largest single shareholder of Franklin Industries and as of now Miss Masterson's the Chairman of the Board of Directors that governs both of them."

She watched those same cock-sucking, two-faced, men who'd, just six months before tried to have her ejected from the building, yet now they applauded her achievements. Those two faced hypocritical pukes. It had been so much fun watching their shocked faces as she went from one to other tapping them on the shoulders and saying, "You're fired, goodbye." When she finished firing nearly all of them, she said, "Would you like me to have security come in to escort you out of the building or can you find your own way out?"

So, it was a done deal. At thirty-eight years old, little Elli Masterson had it all. She'd taken on the big boys and beaten them at their own fucking game and she meant fucking in every sense of the word. This time she got up on the massive desk and stood there with her feet planted firmly apart and asked loudly, "So whose cock of the walk now?"

Now it was time for that drink. She got off the desk, again without falling, sat down on the chair once more, slipped her feet back into her shoes and then pushed the button for that pompous bastard's secretary, Mrs. Patty Vandershot. She was a white haired, fifty-five-year-old, lovely looking woman, who was the best damn executive secretary in the universe. She did what she was told, no matter how much she disagreed with the boss and she did it with gusto, promptly and with style.

The door opened and in walked Mrs. Vandershot, the old battleship.

"Yes, Ma'am, can I help you?" she asked, trying to keep the rancor out of her tone.

"Patty, would you please fix you and me a drink and then have a seat. We have work to do and by the time we're finished, I have a feeling we're going to be friends. I'd like a Rusty Nail and you can have whatever you'd like to drink," Ellie said and yes, she hadn't missed the tone in Vandershot's voice either, but unless she'd missed her guess all that was about to change as well.

"Will that be all, Miss Masterson?" she asked, only this time in a normal tone. Ellie figured that the woman's insides had to be screaming for release of the tight control she had to have been exerting on herself.

"No, and from now on when we're alone anyway, my name's Elli and you are Patty. I want things plain and simple between us and that's an order," Ellie said, playing the game and not giving in to her desire to shout at the woman to chill out and come down off her high horse.

"Yes ma'am. I'll be right back Miss Ellie," Patty said, thinking that Ellie was just toying with her and that made her even madder.

About five minutes later the door opened again and Patty came in with two drinks that she carried on a silver serving tray. Elle came from behind the desk, grabbed her drink and together they took their drinks to a pair of overstuffed leather chairs in a well-appointed conversation corner. Without looking like it, they both watched each other as they sat down opposite from the other, then they carefully placed the drinks on the coffee table between them.

"I suppose you've already heard what I did with the board after the election?" Ellie asked, ready to destroy Patty's preconceived impression of her.

"Yes," Patty replied, still guarded and knowing what was going on, but was determined not to end up out on a limb and handing Ellie the saw.

"Good, now what do you say you take your head out of wherever it's at, at the present time anyway and give me an honest answer. Will you accept the position of VP in charge if Administration? You've got one minute to answer." Ellie watched the wheels at work behind those dark blue eyes and could only guess what was taking place in there. Those eyes changed from guarded to one of shock.

"Yes," Patty shot back at her. She didn't need to think that over. If this was a game, she was going to play it out to the last joker and bet the last chip on the table.

"Great, now then can you find me a secretary that's as good as you are or almost as good anyway?" Elle asked and meant it. Patty was nothing but the best at whatever she did. And Ellie was right in her assumptions because Patty felt that if this woman was on the up-and-up, she had just made a new friend.

"Yes," Patty replied. She could only hope that she'd be able to find one and she'd do her damndest to fulfill that answer and make it the truth. She kept her eyes on Ellie to watch her reactions.

"Then do so and while you're at it, you may need one for yourself. That's because as of this very moment your job is to keep my ass out of the soup. You know more about how to run this company than any other person alive and we both know it. If I'm not doing something that I should be doing, then tell me or at least give me a heads up. We both know I'm sort of out of my league here, but between us we're going to trim this dinosaur down to size and ride it for all it's worth. Speaking of worth, what was that brokedick Jeffries making before I fired him?"

"Two hundred and seventy-one per." Meaning the administrative VP was making two hundred and seventy-one thousand dollars per year and that was with full benefits. By this time Patty was answering automatically and as honestly as she could.

"That's good. As of now, you're getting two hundred and ninety-five with benefits. Make out the necessary paperwork and I'll sign it." That did it, Patty was convinced.

The change in Patty attitude was visible and instantaneous. It was as if a bright light suddenly came on in her face and she realized that all this had become real to her. She'd came to work this morning making sixty-eight grand a year and was going home with two ninety-five. Ellie had her first convert and it was time to show Ellie that she was worth what she was paying her.

"Then my first suggestion to you is to rehire Anderson, he's a good man. For years he's been suggesting things and making changes to improve this company, only to have them reversed by the man whose place you're taking. For the last couple of years he's sat there in meetings taking whatever Bennington dished out, but I knew he didn't like it," Patty suggested. Charlie Anderson had been the VP in charge of Production, that is he was up until this morning when she fired everyone.

"Alright, but let him stew for a while. This afternoon find him wherever he's at and set up an appointment for five minutes after nine in the morning. Fix up a one-year contract for him and give him a three percent raise that becomes effective when he signs. Also put him back on the board and give him full autonomy in production. So long as it continues to produce our product, he has a job. We need an out too, put that in the contract just in case this doesn't work out. This is good stuff Patty, any other suggestions?"

"I know a guy who'd make a great advertising VP," Patty suggested. She'd know Sal for years and knew he'd jump at the chance to come in, but he was somewhat of a wildcard at times. Still, all in all, he was a good Add man.

"Thanks, but I know a woman who'd make an even greater Advertising VP," Ellie said, making Patty drop her train of thought. "She's buried over at GM and chomping at the bit to break out of their corporate mold. I think she'd kill for a chance to be our Advertising VP. Fix up a contract for her, giving her the same money as that prick Hanks was making and word it like Charlie's. Unless I say otherwise, all contracts are on a yearly basis."

"Mine too?" Patty asked.

"Yes. Patty, you need to get it into your head that I expect you set up your own staff and unlike the previous CEO, this one doesn't care what gender the person is. If they can do the job, they've got one." It was time to start laying down new rules.

Patti really liked the sound of that. Her two years at Vassar were finally going to start paying off. She took a sip of her drink and actually tasted it. Glancing out the window, it suddenly seemed like a much brighter day. She turned her full attention back to Ellie and knew come hell or high water; she'd get a second contract.

"Is there anything pressing today that I can't get out of?" Elli asked.

"No, but Marston is coming in from Toronto tomorrow for lunch and your meeting with him was scheduled for the first two hours of the afternoon." Jay Marston was the CEO of their Canadian division. By having a small plant in Canada, that gave them a backdoor access to England and all of Europe.

"What's he after, do you know?" Ellie fished.

"Yes, since the Canadian Division's been making a steady rise in profits and product reliability, they're looking for a larger slice of the pie," Patty said, remembering the memos that crossed her desk.

"OK, schedule some time to give me a complete run down after my meeting with Charlie in the morning, then we can bring him in. Anything else?" Ellie asked. She was going to make this work and finally her screwy, open ideas on running a company would be used. She was determined to make them work or die trying.

"Nothing that can't wait," Patty said, looking at Ellie's tired face and this time she was seeing the strain of the past week showing itself. Ellie was exhausted.

"Good, then set everything else back to next week. And another thing, from now on I want you in on all labor relations issues. Let's make our employees a little happier and give them an incentive to be working for us. I also want you to set up an appointment with someone who can build us a state of the art Product Development Department. It's time we took these types of computers out of the basement and put them on the top shelf," she said, thinking aloud.

Patty got up and left Ellie sitting there staring at the company logo over the fireplace.

Franklin Industries made computers for operating systems, systems like those that ran cars and trucks as well as for other machinery components, stuff like automated assembly lines. The beauty of their computers was the fact they could be programmed differently for each and every application they were used in. If a person wanted his car to run faster and shift differently, the computer would allow for the change to be made by its owner, that is if he bought an advanced chip from Franklin Industries and installed it over the existing chip that the auto manufacturer had installed. Since introducing their specialized computer for cars in the late seventies, Franklin Industries had developed rapidly, but here of late they had been growing stagnant, nothing new was on the horizon.

Nowadays, with the advent of personal computers, notebooks and hi-tech iPhones making inroads into how vehicles were handled and operated, it was time to change again or they would disappear altogether. Companies like On-Star and Sat-Com were putting their own computers into the vehicles and unless something was done immediately, Franklin would be on the outside looking in. Then there were the special entertainment systems that were being introduced as add-ons. They were good to go for the present, but what about next year?

Ellie knew all this and when she'd came to that prick, Peters, with her ideas he stole them and threw her out after asking for another quick fuck. Ellie remembered that and it was such a sweet moment this morning when she'd fired him along with the rest of those men. She did this less than five minutes after the reading of the votes.

Yes, she'd come a long way from Toledo University where she'd studied business administration, media advertising and accounting. She remembered the graduation day as though it was this morning. She also remembered having to fuck her career advisor, he was the first one to use her the same way most men did. But the problem was that they didn't use her mind, they only used her body.

Chapter Two

"Mrs. Samuels, send my next student in," the voice was coming from a box on the secretary's desk. Ellie was already getting up when the secretary motioned for her.

"Mr. Turner will see you now," Mrs. Samuels said absentmindedly, while picking up another stack of papers from her in-box.

Ellie gathered her books into her arms and when in.

"Come in, Miss Masterson and take a seat. I see you want to be a businessperson when you graduate and by the looks of it, you're taking the right courses. Any idea what field you want to be a businessperson in?" he asked, looking intently at her. But Ellie'd seen that look on men before and she knew what he wanted right from the get-go.

"I prefer to be called a businesswoman and I want to work in the electronics field. My two brothers taught me how to fix a radio when I was seven and I've gotten better at it over the years, however I don't want to be in production, I want to be in administration. That's where the money's at," she said, trying to keep this as professional as she could.

"You seem quite focused. Do you have a target company?" He played the game, but it was easy to see the type of game he was playing by how he looked at her.

"No, not yet. I was hoping you might suggest one," She said, giving into him and hoping to get her way.

A week later she was a frequent visitor to his office, but it was not to go over her career, it was to drop her jeans and bend over the desk. Sure, she was furthering her career, but not with her mind. However, it'd been Samuel who'd gotten her in the side door at Franklin and she guessed she should thank him for that, but she wouldn't. She felt too dirty.

The evening after graduation she stood in front of the mirror, focused her light brown eyes on the image and tried to see what men saw when they looked at her. Did she have some sort of mark on her that symbolized she was available to them?

Her short, auburn hair didn't look any different than anyone else's. At that time it was feathered, slightly curled and only about three inches long, exposing her ears. Those dainty ears were tight against her head and she kept diamond studs in them all the time. Her mother had given them to her when her grandmother died and she never took them out. A long neck supported her well-shaped head and held it up proudly.

Was it her unblemished skin that turned the men on? Early on in her life she knew that even a tiny tattoo would destroy the perfection that her Maker had bestowed upon her so she resisted the temptation to get one like the other girls were doing. Maybe it was her large hazel eyes or was it her upturned nose, her generous lips or maybe her stubborn chin? It had to be something. She unbuttoned her blouse and looked at her breasts. They were generously proportioned and maybe a little too full for her frame, but she kept them as unobtrusive as she could with her bra selections. She had an in-se bellybutton and a waist so small that a man with large hands could almost encircle it with them. A twenty-one-inch waist was something to be proud of in this day in age.

Dropping her blouse, she looked at her hips. They were full and if she had an inviting feature about her that was it. Turning sideways she looked at the protrusion of her butt and like her hips, it too demanded attention. Therefore, to Ellie, if she was going to un-advertise her sexuality she would have to wear clothes that disguised the size and shape of her butt, and still toned down her hips, but how was she going to do that?

Then came those legs, she had a thirty-inch inseam when she bought jeans and she figured that for some reason those legs seemed to signal something to the male of the species as well. If she wore dresses to hide her ass, they'd show her legs. Pants would take the legs out of the equation, but what was she going to do with her ass then? It was hell being so damn well built. Perhaps if she went to a good dress shop, maybe they could help her? That was the ticket, but they cost money and it was money she didn't have, YET!

After her shower she sat on a high stool in the kitchen, leaned on the counter in front of her and continued with her train of thought. There was another possibility, she could keep her legs closed and end the dilemma, but who was she kidding. This was a man's world and even at this late day in age, women were only good for one thing as far as a man was concerned. In the "Fortune Five Hundred", there were only two companies, so far, that had a woman as their CEO. Two out of the five hundred wasn't a very good average.

Even as this country approached the new millennium, women who were built like Ellie were used for only one thing. Oh sure, they were promised this and given a token that, but in the end it was the man who got to be the company president or CEO. It seemed like no amount of sex or knowledge on the woman's part could break through that invisible barrier. Ellie knew that and she decided that very day to go as far up the ladder as she could get, and she'd get there by using any means available to her. She pulled out her short skirt, a sweater blouse and nude colored pantyhose and put them on. It was time to give them what they wanted.

~♥~

That had been fifteen years ago and the list of men who'd used her body over the next several years to make themselves feel powerful was long and distinguished, but the bottom line was this, she was now sitting in the catbird's seat. Ellie got up and went behind the desk, but before she sat down she unfastened the garter belt she had on and pulled it from her body. She looked at the offending article of clothing and openly hated it. To her it represented one of the conditions for her continued employment at Franklin, by men of course, but if she had her way it never would again. If she had her way, she'd ban them from ever being worn anywhere, but she wouldn't or couldn't do that, it was, after all, a woman's prerogative to wear whatever she wanted. Men had that right, why not extend that option to women.

She sat down and as she did she dropped the garment into the trashcan. Slipping her shoes off again, she rolled the nylons down and they found themselves in the trashcan along with the belt. Feeling emancipated, she put her bare feet on the desk and it felt wonderful. Fuck tradition, decorum and modesty, she was the head mother in charge and she didn't have to answer to anyone, not anymore, her ass-kissing days were over.

Sitting up and putting her feet under the desk, she hit the button for the intercom again. She was surprised to hear a strange voice answer her secretary's call.

"Yes, Ma'am," came the soft voice.

"Bring your pad and come in here," Ellie said. It was time for her to let the working people know she was in charge.

"Yes, ma'am."

Two seconds later the door opened and a woman came in who looked like a heavier version of Patty. She had short gray hair and everything.

In answer to Ellie's questioning look, the woman said, "I'm Roberta Winthrop, your new secretary."

"Do you have a nick name or any other name you go by?"

"Yes, ma'am. Bobbie."

"Alright, Bobby. I'm Ellie and when we're alone use it, but I'd appreciate you calling me by my formal name when others are in here. Take a seat and relax, Bobbie. We're about to make history.

She began talking and as she did Bobby was kept busy writing it all down on her pad using shorthand, something she hadn't used for years.

"From this moment on there will be a dress code in force for this firm. The men who work for this company are to wear business suits for executives, sport coats and slacks for foremen and supervisors and blue colored jeans for workers. Women, on the other hand, can wear anything they want, within prudent standards that is. When we're finished here, fix that up and bring it in for my signature.

"Next item. I want a suggestion box placed in every department and a form made up for their usage. Any employee who comes up with a good suggestion on how to better production, sales, or boost anything associated with this company will be automatically placed on the list for advancement in their departments or one similar to it. Suggestions concerning administration or personnel matters will receive a bonus payment of not less than one hundred dollars and not more than a thousand.

"Next item. Every building owned by Franklin will have a daycare center built into them and employees who use the facilities will be charged to total of one dollar per child per hour for the time that the child stays in the centers. Make a note to mention this to Patty and set this up with her. I want the centers to be open twenty-four hours a day.

"Final item. Anyone who uses one of the new van's that we're going to acquire, they will be for their transportation to-and-from work, will receive an incentive of two cents per hour in their pay. Over a hundred of these vans will be bought in the next two months."

Bobbie took a few moments to go over her notes before she stood up and left. She held her head up a little higher when she did and if truth be known, she had a hint of humor in her eyes.

When the door closed, Ellie said to no one, "That should raise a few eyebrows."

She got up, stood at the window of the top floor office and looked out at the Ann Arbor skyline. Off in the distance she could see the Michigan University Stadium and remembered that limpdick, visiting executive that she'd had to give a hand-job to under the blanket that he held over their legs. This year she was going to use the company's luxury box in that very same stadium, it was on the fifty-yard line and there would be no more hand-jobs while she was running this company. Not by her, not by any woman who worked for her and if she caught anyone doing it, she'd make their lives miserable. She was the last woman in this company who was going to have to screw her way to the top. They'd have to make it by merit and merit alone.

Chapter Three

Nash opened and arranged two more six-packs of beer in the cooler and then closed the ice chests lid. He knew he'd have to run extra laps to burn off all the calories he'd be consuming this weekend, but what the hell. This annual campout was one of his favorite forms of relaxation. The get-together with his old U of M football chums was always fun. No women, no kids and no stops of any sort either.

He remembered the year one of them brought a prostitute with him, although she was not screwed by any of them. Instead, she was promptly paid her fee, given a bonus and sent on her way, along with the man who'd brought her up to the campgrounds in the first place. For the next three years he was excluded from the three-day bash, so, women were defiantly out.

Fishing, boating, waterskiing, water jetting, horseshoes, volleyball, and just plain lounging around was the name of the game for them. Besides, most of them were married with kids and they didn't need any problems of that sort. So, no women allowed, that was the name of the game.

Nash Gibson was still single; not divorced and even after all these years, he was still the brunt of a lot of teasing by the others and talked about in closed circles. He'd been called everything from being a fag, to being dead from the waist down. However, anyone who knew Nash, also knew that he wasn't hurting in the women department. He was outdoorsy handsome; tall, at least six-three and built like a Greek God. At thirty-nine years old he still had a full head of almost black hair and no gray strands, --- yet. His friends complained that he was having it replanted every year, but it was all his and it was natural.

The drive up to the campgrounds took him about four hours. The small camp was reserved for them and only them over the three-day weekend of Memorial Day every year. They paid top dollar for this privilege, but it was worth it. The Lake Michigan campground was directly on a sandy beach that was a little off to one side of the Mackinaw Straits. It was at the end of a private secondary road and to say it was secluded would be underselling it, this place was downright remote.

"Hey, Nash, you want to go fishing with us?" Jay shouted from the pier. He was standing up in an eighteen-foot speedboat and Hank was sitting at the controls. If he knew Hank, there'd be very little fishing done today and a whole lot of drinking.

"Naw, I'm going to take a dip and then lay in the sun for a while to warm up. Besides, Terry and I have the duty tonight." Everyday two men's names were drawn out of a hat and they did the cooking, while two others cleaned up afterwards. Nash was doing the cooking tonight and he planned to surprise them, shrimp-ka-bobs were going to be his donation to this evening's meal. Terry was cooking some nice steaks and baked potatoes to go with them. Of course, an ocean of beer would be consumed by them as well, but then why not, they were on vacation.

Only there was something was wrong with Nash tonight; he didn't feel like getting drunk again. After supper and the others were cleaning up, he walked down the beach to watch the sunset over the water. He found a washed-up tree trunk half buried in the sand, sat down and listened to the waves lap the beach. It bothered him as he began to wonder if he was ever going to become as successful as some of the other guys from the team were. He slid down the log and sat on the still warm sand, while leaning back against the log and relaxing.

His career was at a logger-jam and for the last three years, all he'd gotten was cost of living raises at his present job. He was still creative and turned out good product, it's just that he was spinning his wheels and was getting nowhere fast. Maybe he needed a change of scenery, like Todd did. Eight months ago his friend Todd had sold his small manufacturing business and converted a small company completely to Internet Product Distribution. In the last six months he'd had to expand twice.

But what would he, mister solid and dependable Nash Gibson, do if he quit the design department at GM. Two of his designs were on the road now and another due out in two years. He made a hundred and seventy grand a year and lived comfortably, so why was he complaining and thinking about rocking the boat? Maybe he was expecting too much of himself? Nevertheless, his idea of creating a car that would drive completely on its own, autonomously, never left his head. The GM bigwigs had looked at his suggestions and then promptly said it would never be practical, then they sent him a rejection notice and then shelved the idea. It was a good idea though and one that he'd perfected over this past year. He had six hundred grand saved in securities, but he figured that a project like this would take millions upon millions to develop and produce properly, maybe even billions.

Nash heard the guys shouting about something and looked up to see them carrying Mac down to the lake. They took him out on the dock and tossed him in, clothes and all. That was the gang's punishment for any and all infractions of the party mode. Mac must have talked about work again, causing him to get a dunking. It occurred to him that if he didn't get out of the thinking mode that he was in, he'd be the next one off the end of the pier. He picked his half-empty beer can up and headed for the campfire to join the others.

~♥~

Monday morning, Memorial Day, found him out in the middle of the Straits in one of the boats fishing with Charlie Anderson. Charlie was a good guy, smart as hell and he worked for Franklin Industries as an executive VP of some department there. He was in charge of something or other and making headway towards the top spot in the company, at least according to him he was.

A boat went by with three women in it and Charlie said, "That reminds me, I'm now working for a woman. I think she looks like the one who's driving that fucking boat over there." He pointed to the receding boat and said, "You're not going to turn me in are you. For three years, I've avoided the annual dunking by you guys."

"No, Charlie, your transgression's safe with me. You feel like talking about it, you go right ahead and talk," Nash said.

"Last week this woman was made CEO and Board President of Franklin. However, the board went one-step further and put her in control of the foundation too. That means she can't be voted out of the office she's in now unless she wants to be. Everyone knows she slept her way to the top and the first thing this bitch does is fire everyone on the board, me included. Then, the next morning she calls me in and hires me back under a one-year contract and then gives me a three percent pay raise. Shit, that's more of a raise than I've gotten in six years. She also put me back on the board and gave me a free hand in production. She's actually doing some good in and for the plant too. Daycare centers in all the buildings are just one of the innovations she's instituting."

"So, what's the complaint?"

"She never screwed me to get where she's at and that's one good looking broad. Whoever thought that someday she'd be our boss? Not me, that's for damn sure. For-Christ-sake, she started out as a fucking secretary and now she's the head mother in charge."

"Is she married? Does she have any kids?"

"Shit no. In the first place who'd marry the executive lounge tramp? I guess I should consider myself lucky I didn't screw her, every one that did screw her got fired this week."

"How many was that?"

"Over twenty and that's a conservative estimate."

Nash looked at his friend and said, "Let me give you a little food for thought. Since graduating U of M, I'll bet you I've slept with over a hundred women and I'm still single. Why is it bad for a woman to sleep with a man, but not bad for a man to sleep with a woman? Think about it?"

"You or her, you could sleep with whoever you want, but when you select a man or a woman with the sole intention of screwing them to advance your position within a department, that's called, at least in my book, being a whore. My friend, what you do is recreational screwing and if a woman did that kind of fucking, I wouldn't look down on her either. There's a difference."

"So, what's this bitch look like?" Nash asked.

"She's absolutely gorgeous, long legs, big hooters, great ass, slender waist, long neck and perfect face and hair. She'd make Pamela Anderson Lee set up and take notice. Baywatch would have killed to have a woman who looks like this on their show."

"Well then, what's the problem?"

"For one thing, I've never worked for a woman before. My wife's seen her and she doesn't like me working with her, but so far this bitch has done everything right. I guess I'll just have to wait and see."

"By the sounds of this, I need to meet this babe."

"She'd eat you up and spit you out for breakfast. You don't need this sort of hell in your life. I've got a feeling she's nothing but poison and I'm watching my back."

"So, what you're saying is that you like her and you don't like her. That you respect her and your wife hates her. But you'll stay on and see where she takes you, is that about it?"

"You got it, Nash old boy. I can't afford to do anything else."

It wasn't until Nash was driving home later on that night, that he thought about Charlie's dilemma again. Having a wife nagging at him at home would kill a guy like Charlie so it looked like a position would be opening up with Franklin shortly. But, did he want to put himself in a position to work for a woman like this? Maybe he should go in there and sleep his way to the top if she was that damn good looking. Besides, he liked screwing and he wasn't all that that choosy about with whom, but he did have standards on what she looked like.

Chapter Four

"Bobby, get Udall up here for me. Tell him I want to go over our legal rights to several properties that we have," Ellie shouted out the open door of her office. Don Udall was the company's top lawyer and he headed a department that employed six more of those legal sharks.

"Yes, ma'am. By the way there is a Mr. Nash Gibson who called and asked if he could set up an appointment to see you. He works for GM and wants to talk to you about an idea he has for a project."

"Did he say what that project was?" Ellie asked.

"No, ma'am. But he did say you'd like it."

"OK, if he calls again, give him fifteen minutes Friday before noon. I'd like to run away this weekend and my cabin on Black Lake is sounding better and better as this week goes on. Did Mattie check in?" Mattie Sanders was her new VP of Advertising, the one she enticed away from Ford.

"Yes, she'll be in at three. She says she's got good news, but it's a surprise," Bobbie said, as she came in and took the papers out of Ellie's "Out" basket.

"Great!" Ellie said and rolled her eyes to the ceiling.

Ten minutes later Bobbie called her on the intercom and said, "You've got Mr. Gibson at eleven-thirty on Friday."

"Thanks Bobbie," Ellie said. She was very happy with Patties selection for a private secretary for her, Bobby was everything she'd been and sometimes more, but never better.

~♥~

When Mattie came storming into the building at five after three shouting hellos to everyone she knew, she went directly into Ellie's office and was barely able to contain her exuberance; she beamed from top to bottom. Standing there, she bounced on the balls of her feet.

"Come, set over here. I don't want you to go throwing the papers off your desk all around your office," Mattie said as she bounded over and sat down on the edge of her seat.

"What the hell have you done now?" Ellie inquired, as she took her seat.

Mattie jumped up, put a DVD in the machine and turned on the TV. The DVD began to play and a few moments later the crest of Franklin Industries came on the screen. Ellie sat and watched the thirty-second add play out. It was professionally done, well thought out and it expounded on Franklin Industries itself. It was about how they were leading the industry into the Twenty-First Century through technology and it implied that they were looking towards the Twenty-Second Century already.

"That's nothing to be excited about. It's good, I'll grant you that, but so what. That's your job," Ellie said, looking at Mattie.

"What if I told you I've got a copy of that tape and one more exactly like that, that they will be playing twice in the first hour of the Super Bowl?" she asked excitedly.

"My God, you do? How in the hell'd you do that and what's it costing us?" Now Ellie was excited as well.

"Chryslers giving it to us for a three-year contract on our new engine computer and at its present cost. I told them it was up to you, but that I was sure you'd go along with it."

The commercial had to be costing them from between one and two million dollars, but the beauty of it was it wouldn't appear on any sheet of paper as an advertising expenditure. The PR alone with a spot like that was enormous. No one could get any sort of commercial spot anywhere for the next six or seven Super Bowls.

"Good job. Go over this with Don and make sure we're not doing anything illegal," Ellie said.

"We've also got four seats in their private box. Want to go to a football game?"

"Not unless the Detroit Lions makes it. I'll keep it in mind though. Anything else?" Ellie asked.

"Nope, but I'd sure like to thank you again for getting me out of perdition." She got up and left the office. Ellie went back behind her desk and thought about the game. Just to say you were there was important in this business. She made up her mind, she was going no matter who was in the Super Bowl.

For this meeting today, Nash wore a gray cashmere sport coat over his dark blue shirt, a light gray tie and Levi's. A penny-loafers style of shoe completed his ensemble for his introduction to the CEO of Franklin. If he was guessing right and could seriously take Charlie's word for anything, this woman might just be interested in his ideas.

He packed his papers and other things in an expandable folder so everything would be in the right order when he pulled them out and then carefully tied it shut, no briefcase today. It bothered him to taking the day off from work to see her, but what the hell, something had to give. He had never been the sort of man who could stand still for long, he had to move forward or stop altogether.

Parking in the guest space off to the side of the Piedmont Building, he went inside and walked up to the uniformed guard behind the circular desk inside the door.

"Mr. Gibson to see Miss Masterson," he announced, stopping at the desk.

The guard punched some keys on a computer and read what was on the screen.

"Yes, Sir, she's expecting you. Take elevator number four to the twenty-second floor. The office is to the left of the elevator door and it's marked CEO."

As Nash rode up in the elevator, he thought about the directions given by the guard. The man made sure he got it in that she was CEO. By the looks of things they were all plying the game of 'Keep My Job'. He began to rethink his idea of coming here to pitch his brainchild, especially if she was that shallow. He remembered his conversation with Charlie out there on the lake two months ago and then he forced his mind to focus on tomorrow's game between U of M and Penn State to make it relax a little. This game was going to be a good one and his season's ticket next to Charlie would defiantly get used this year. It was finally turning cool outside and it was perfect football weather.

The doors opened and he turned left. The décor was rich looking. Directly in front of the elevator was an open door marked Development. Inside, construction was going on, they were building a new department. This looked promising.

He pushed one of the double glass doors open and stepped into some sort of combination secretary's office and a waiting room. There was rich comfortable furniture placed around the room, expensive looking paintings hung on the wallpapered walls and there were three secretaries' sitting behind desks, all of them were working away at their computers. One of them looked up and asked, "Good morning, may I help you, Sir."

"Yes, Mr. Gibson to see Miss Masterson."

"Please go through that door. Miss Masterson's secretary is expecting you."

She turned her attention back to her keyboard and seemingly ignored him. He went to the door and opened it. This was a smaller version of the large outer office, but there were some subtle differences. The desks in here was richer looking, the carpet thicker, the paintings on the walls were originals, the furniture was more luxurious and this secretary was dressed in the sort of clothes that didn't come off the rack at K-Mart.

"Good morning, Mr. Gibson. Would you like a cup of coffee while you're waiting to see Miss Masterson?" It was a polite way of telling him to have a seat and wait.

"No thank you, I'm fine."

He sat down next to an eight-foot high tree and picked up a magazine off the table. When he looked at it, he was surprised; it was the current issue of Playboy. Feeling a little uncomfortable looking at it, he put the book back on the table and watched the secretary instead. She worked efficiently at her computer terminal without paying any mind to him. Her desk was relatively clear of other papers. All that was on it was a PBX phone, the computer monitor with keyboard and a silver holder full of pens and markers. On one corner was an 'in' basket made of wood that matched the desk.

Suddenly she stopped typing and said, "Miss Masterson will see you now." She got up and went to the door on the other side of where she sat and opened it for him. As he went by the desk, he wondered how she knew her boss was ready to see him. A question to be answered at some other date, right now he had more important fish to fry.

Franklin's CEO was standing in front of her desk when he came in; she held out her hand and said with a smile, "Good morning,

Mr. Gibson. Why don't we set over here, I'm sure we'll be more comfortable?"

She walked in front of him to a pleasant setting arranged around a fireplace and she took a seat on the couch while adjusting her skirt and crossing her ankles just so as she sat down. She was wearing a light gray business cut jacket and a skirt ensemble that looked like a suit and it showed off her frilly white silk blouse. But that was the last hint that the person seated there was a woman, in fact she acted like he expected the CEO of a major company to act. She wore her auburn hair loose and it fell down across her shoulders in soft curls, not a single strand was out of place. The hair framed her lovely face, pouty lips, wide set hazel eyes and it hid about half of her ears. Like her hair, the dress she wore hid most of her charms, but nothing could conceal those long wonderful legs.

"Did Bobby fix you up with coffee? She makes a divine cappuccino," Ellie asked.

"She asked, but I declined. Let me get right to it, I'm sure your time is valuable and I don't want to take up any more of it than I have to." He figured, and rightly so, that he was under a time constraint and he wanted to get as much of this out as he could.

Ellie leaned back on the couch and turned her attention to the strikingly handsome man that was sitting across from her. Why couldn't some of those pricks she'd had to screw to get where she was now look like this, she asked herself. She put those sorts of thoughts from her head and listened to his pitch.

For fifteen minutes she listened to his proposal and when Bobby came in to remind her of her next appointment, thus ending this one for her, she said, "Thank you. Is he here yet?"

"Yes Ma'am."

"Tell him that I'll be a few minutes," Ellie said, standing up, thus ending the meeting. Bobby left and closed the door.

"Mr. Gibson, do you like football?" she asked, making up her mind on the spur of the moment.

"Yes, Ma'am. I played for the University of Michigan for four years while I was getting my degree," Nash said as he finished putting his papers in the folder and standing up.

"Are you going to the game tomorrow?" she inquired.

"Yes, Ma'am, wouldn't miss it. Are you going?" he asked, looking up at her. Something in the sound of her voice told him things had changed and he wanted to see the expression on her face.

"How would you like to watch the game with me in our box? Then, during halftime, you can finish your presentation. Your idea intrigues me and I'd like to hear more about it."

"Can do! Which box is it?" he asked enthusiastically thinking that he wasn't dead yet.

"Number seventy. I'll leave word at the door for them to let you up. See you tomorrow."

"You won't regret it, Miss Masterson. This idea will not only fly, it'll work and make your company millions in profits."

"I think we can jump ahead to calling each other by our given names. Mine's Ellie."

"I'm Nash and I'll see you tomorrow, Ellie," he said as he walked towards the door.

"Nash, would you please use that door," she indicated a door on the opposite wall.

When he went through the door, he was standing in an elevator lobby. It was a small lobby and as soon as he pushed the down button, the doors opened. This elevator was smaller and when the doors opened again he was standing in a short hall that led to the side of the building; he was right next to where he'd parked. This meant that she most likely had her own private entrance and by having the people who came in to see her use it, the next person waiting in line to see her never saw who she'd seen before them. That was a great idea. Now then, all he had to do is be smart enough to get to see this elevator again. In the parking lot he turned and looked back at the impressive building and thought about that woman he'd just met, she acted like a CEO but looked like a centerfold from that magazine he'd picked up in her secretary's office. What a combination.

Chapter Five

It was after seven that evening when Ellie let herself into her home on Bridgeway Drive, it was right next to the Country Clubs Golf Course. The house was a huge colonial style mansion complete with eight massive columns out front holding up a portico that extended over part of the driveway. It even had a fountain in the center of the circular driveway. This was the house she'd inherited when she became involved with the old coot that set her up in the first place. She'd been living there for nearly a month, it was hers, in fact it had been left to her in the old mans will when he died.

The entire estate hid behind an eight-foot-high stone-wall that had been built for privacy. It also hid her outside pool and tennis court from any stray eyes from the golf course. There was a six-car garage alongside the house, with servant's quarters over it and another pool inside that was surrounded with glass that also housed a hot tub and sauna, they were there for whiling away the long Michigan winters in comfort.

Ellie only had two people working for her at the present time, a maid and a grounds keeper who doubled as her chauffeur when she went out as a CEO. She was still working at filling up the library walls with the right sorts of books, books that she'd eventually read, sometime, and Gina, her maid, was helping her.

Gina was a find, she'd found her working in the factory part of Franklin Industries producing computers. It was actually Patty who found her and two days after she'd interviewed Gina, Gina moved into one of the mansions domestic cottages over the garage.

Jerome Redman, her chauffeur, was a tall black-man and at one time he'd played basketball for the Detroit Piston's for part of a season, but had both of his knees blown out during the second game he played. This unfortunate event happened when he was pushed into the stands trying to retrieve a rebound. After six weeks in the hospital and rehab, he was released when the doctors told him he'd never play again; in fact they told him that he was lucky to be walking. For a while Jerome was mad at the world, but by his second trip to the Wayne County Jail for fighting, he had gotten over that crap. His parole officer was the one who recommended him for the job that Ellie had submitted a request for, it was with the Michigan Employment Office and she did this when she took possession of the house. Within a week after coming to work here, he was happy again and singing as he worked in the yard or was busy around the pool keeping the leaves out of it. On his days off he seldom left the grounds, electing to stay in his room next to Gina's reading some of the books from Ellie's growing library. His tenacity for seeking knowledge was unending, that is once he got started and of course Ellie encouraged this.

When Gina heard the front door close, she came in to take Ellie's handbag and jacket. "You look tired; want me to draw you a bath before you set down to supper?"

"No, what'd you fix tonight?" Ellie asked, as she sat down on the park-like bench in the foyer to remove her shoes.

"A spinach chief's salad with honey cured ham and that cheese you like."

"Have you and Jerome already eaten?" she asked leaning back and relaxing.

"No, we were waiting for you. You sure you don't want me to draw you a bath?"

"I'll be fine, Gina. Put it on the table while I check the mail, anything good come today?"

"There's a letter there from your folks and a postcard from Brenda in Japan."

Ellie was in the main foyer, but in reality it was more like a three-story high atrium. After kicking her shoes off, she walked over to the small table near the foot of the curved grand staircase and picked up the letters. With the mail in hand, she took the letters into the study next to the staircase and sat at an ornate Louie the Fifteenth desk. This room was all dark wood, including the cross-bucked ceiling.

After reading the postcard, she opened the letter from her mom. Her dad was dying of cancer and as soon as she took over Franklin, she made certain that he got into the best nursing home she could find. It was one that allowed her mother to live there with him, but his bedroom was more like a hospital room. Ellie was upset that she couldn't spend any more time with them than she did, but she always kept Sundays open for her dad.

"Honey, your dad's gotten worse and now he doesn't recognize anyone. He eats, but only a little. I hope God takes him soon while he's asleep and makes his suffering stop. I don't know what we'd have done if you hadn't found this place. It's going to make his last few months on this earth a lot more comfortable and easy. And it's making life for me easier too. The nurses are wonderful, but I see the futility in their eyes every time I look at them. I look forward to seeing you Sunday so I'll close for now. Love, Mom and Dad."

Ellie reread the letter and put it back in the envelope. After reading something like that, it sure put a damper on her Friday night. She wondered if her trek to power had been worth what she'd had to pay in order to get there, but she simply had to look around her and read that letter again to know it had been.

She got up and went into the kitchen to have supper with Jerome and Gina.

~♥~

After his meeting with Ellie, Nash figured that Charlie was off in his estimation of this woman's abilities by a country mile. Following this meeting with Ellie, Nash could only shake his head in amazement and he did this at both her beauty and her business savvy. He noticed that all during the meeting she had asked pointed questions about specific aspects of his idea and she was a lot more knowledgeable than any man or woman that he knew, even if they thought they were smart and well informed. If Charlie dreamt he was going to move into her position when she failed, he'd be worm bait by the time that happened. Ellie was on top of things, even the most current ideas of the day.

When the meeting first began, Nash had a hard time keeping his mind on what he was there for, his eyes kept drifting to those legs, her beautiful face and the perfect hair. However, after the pleasantries were over and they got down to business, he was hard pressed to stay ahead of her and to top it off he was giving his own presentation, one she'd never heard before.

By the time he got to the gym that afternoon to work off some of his frustrations, he was more than ready for this physical release. And besides, he thought better running than he did sitting down. One thing was for certain, this woman was in a class all by herself. As he made laps around the gym, he lost count of them while his mind worked overtime trying to come up with better answers for any questions she might fire at him during the game tomorrow, at least better than what he gave her today. He'd already forgotten what Charlie said about her sleeping her way to the top, this woman was far too smart for her not to be at the top of the heap no mater where she went.

He stripped off his sweaty things and put them in the basket for the gym staff to get them cleaned and that way they'd be ready for him the next time he came there. He grabbed his towel and paddled naked towards the shower for a quick rinse off before heading to the sauna. Later, while sitting there in the sauna with sweat dripping off him, he continued to contemplate what he was going to do and say tomorrow. Then he wondered if she was inviting him as a man or a business colleague? If it was for him to be a man, how was he going to handle it? What did she really have in that pretty head of hers? She fascinated him and scared the living shit out of him at the same time. In her position as CEO, she could make or break him, but she was a ravishing looking woman and she was one he'd like to know better. One thing he did know for sure, he was going to take it slow with this jaguar.

Well here it was, already a month after that bitch ousted him and he was still unemployed. Fray had never been out of work for more than a few days since he was fifteen. Yet, no one wanted a sixty-five-year-old has-been running their companies anymore, not in this day in age anyway. Word of how she'd ousted him had spread around the industry like wildfire and doors that had been open to him a short while ago were closed now. Fray Bennington was on the outside looking in and this sort of treatment was foreign to him.

"That fucking cunt wasn't even a good lay, but she did give good head," he said to the mirror in the bathroom of his new apartment. Two weeks after that bitch had fired him and without any warning his wife of five years went to the bank, took a million eight-hundred-thousand dollars out of their mutual savings account leaving him with measly twelve grand. Then she also took over a million dollars in negotiable stocks from their safety deposit box before the bitch took off and then filed for divorce. On top of that, she had the county sheriff come and throw him out of his own home because, like it was in most mid-western states, that's the way the law reads, it's all geared towards the woman. According to them, she gets the home and he gets the shaft. Moreover, since this was an adultery case, he was considered in the wrong right from the start in the eyes of the law anyway and this was especially true in Michigan. His life was in ruin and getting worse every day.

At least he still had the ten-room cabin up near Houghton Lake and of course there were the millions he'd fleeced from the company over the years, but that money was hidden away in an offshore account where not even his f-ing wife could find it. Nevertheless, he needed a job at one of the car companies or something like that, a job defined him, it sustained him. The million in securities he was left with would never be enough, not for a man like him.

"GOD! Please hold that fucking cocksucking cunt accountable for this; she's the one who really did this to me, not my wife. She did this and should have to pay!" he said aloud while holding his face up next to the mirror and looking deeply into his eyes. They were cruel brown eyes and this was a new look for him.

The next day the huge grandfather clock in the foyer chimed eleven times before Ellie remembered she'd invited a handsome man to join her in the box today for the football game. Ever since getting up at eight this morning and after spending an hour swimming, she thought of nothing except lounging around the house today and maybe even reading a book. Having to go to the game meant she needed to get dressed, not fancy, but at least more than the holey jeans and tee shirt that she was wearing now.

"Gina, would you lay out my Michigan outfit, I'm going to the game today."

"What time are you leaving?" Gina asked.

"One, the game starts at two."

"I'll take Penn and two points," Jerome announced loudly as he came out of the kitchen and stood there in the doorway.

"Shit, so would I if I could find some fool to take that wager, but I'm feeling good today so I'll throw away ten bucks. You're on," Ellie said. Then she stopped and asked, "I thought this was your day off?"

"It is, but I'd rather drive you to the game than sit up there in my room, boss lady."

"Don't try to blow smoke up my ass, what's going on?" she asked, looking at him.

"I broke up with Valerie and I don't feel like going out with anyone else," he replied, revealing his real reason for staying in.

Ellie knew he liked Valerie a lot, but the breakup didn't surprise her. Valerie was another of those sorts of women who hover around powerful, rich or famous men in the hopes of being seen with them. The only way they could become famous themselves was by using their bodies, it was sort of like being high-priced whores. They were shallow and only thought about themselves, and if the truth were known he was better off without her; still, he'd have to get over this on his own.

However, hadn't she done the same thing on her way to the top? NO! She was smart and focused in what she'd done. The only one she really hovered around looking to get ahead with was the company itself. Well, maybe she was like them in a way, but she never hurt any of the men or women on her way to the top. Oh hell, who was she kidding, she was just like them. She'd whored herself and screwed her way to the top, end of discussion.

"Good, you can drive me to the game today and watch Penn lose from my box. I've got a man coming in to talk to me about something so we may be too busy to watch the game with you."

"Deal, boss lady. And after the game you can give me my ten bucks."

If ten bucks was all it took to make him perk-up, it was worth it. She went into the study and sat down at the desk, still thinking about being that kind of woman. Was she really like those girls? She was, except with her, she'd tried to sell her ideas instead of her body, but no one wanted to buy them. Consequently, she'd used her body to get her ideas across, but when that bastard, Fray, stole her ideas and passed them off as his own. In fact, he'd pissed her off so much that nothing could have stopped her from doing what she done. She actually felt bad about nearly screwing that old man half to death, starting in the foundation lobby and working their way to the parking garage, but it had to be that way and the end justified the means, at least in her book it did.

~♥~

Six months ago she'd gone to see the Chairmen of the Board of Trusties of the Franklin Institute to plead with him to intervene, but when the sixty-eight-year-old letch kept trying to look up her dress, she turned her sexuality loose on him. Two days later, while they were lying in his bed naked and he was gasping for a breath of air, she got him to promise to give her the paper transferring the right to vote the seventy-five point five million shares of Franklin Industries that the company owned in a coming proxy fight. After that it was easy, she now had the exclusive voting rights to fifty-five percent of all of Franklin's stock. Did that make her a whore and make her like the other girls, because if it did her payoff was a hell of a lot more than any whore she knew. Her salary now was two-million-five a year with stock options, profit sharing and incentives on top of bonuses. Two weeks after she took over Franklin and attended the old man's funeral, she'd moved into this house thus completing her rise to the top. Money would never be a problem for her again.

But was she a whore? In the truest sense of the word, yes, however, she was a retired whore who would only open her legs for a man that she cared about from here on out. And if he was doing the same thing as she'd done, she hoped that she'd be smart enough to recognize it and then the prick would be sent packing, minus his balls.

Ellie opened the bottom drawer, removed the lockbox and opened it. She took out the white envelope that was holding the voting rights to the foundations shares, she opened the envelope and reread the notarized legal form. It gave her the rights to vote that stock for the rest of her natural life. If she wanted to, she could bring Franklin down, but that wasn't her intention. In fact, she wanted to take them into the rarified heights of being a mega company in this industry. The only way to do that was to diversify and expand with new ideas, that's what she was doing today.

This guy, Nash, had just that type of idea, the sort that would shake up the industry, at least he did in her estimation anyway. If they could develop his idea most auto accidents that happened today would become a thing of the past. Drivers would still drive their cars and trucks, but two onboard servo computers and one master computer that received information from outside the car would take over the car when and if it became endangered. It updated itself thirty times a second and took in information from three hundred and sixty degrees around the car for a distance of one thousand feet. The beauty of this idea was that it saw around corners, through fog and rain and worked at night, even without lights. Whenever danger to the vehicle was perceived, then the cars onboard computers took over its operation and kept it out of danger's way by stopping it or steering it away from potential problems.

This system also had an added benefit, when the driver got in the car he or she could program the computer with their destination and with very little effort on the driver's part, the car could take that person to their destination by using the best route possible. The cars computer recognized road signs, traffic signals, speed bumps and it even saw potholes.

But Ellie wanted to know more about this system, things like its cost per unit, the additional cost to the cars manufacturer, public acceptability, legal ramifications, governmental involvement and any of other dozens of things that would or could possibly prevent this idea from becoming a reality. That's what she was going to discuss with Nash today during the game.

She got up and left the room to go upstairs and get dressed. A boss's work was never done, at least a real bosses wasn't.

Nash thought about dressing in slacks, dress shirt and tie, but instead he put on his faded jeans and a Michigan sweatshirt. It was the same one he'd worn for years and to him it was his and the teams lucky shirt. When he wore it, Michigan didn't lose and by the looks of things, so far this year anyway, they'd need all the help they could get, especially against Penn State today.

As he dressed, he thought about this woman he was going to see today and hopefully finish pitching his idea to her. She was one of the most beautiful women he'd ever seen, but her beauty was strongly overshadowed by her intelligence. This woman was smart and if he didn't stay on his toes, she'd eat him alive. This was the sort of woman who did her homework and he was sure she'd come at him today with questions he had no answers for. With that in mind, he once more began to go over in his mind any possible question she might come up with and the most important of them would be if GM would want a piece of this idea, because technically he worked for them when this idea was hatched and he'd proposed it to them first. The fact that they'd turned him down was important, but he had no hard proof of what they had done with his idea. All he had was the rejection notice, ---, wait--- that was it, the rejection notice.

He remembered a memo he'd sent to Roger Vanderman last year, Roger was the VP in charge of development. Roger had written his ideas on the bottom of the memo before it was sent it back to him and it stated that Nash's idea was impractical for this companies' image, and that GM didn't want any part of it. Jumping up, Nash headed for his closet to find that memo and the rejection notice. Once more he was back on track and happy.

Chapter Six

The game was scheduled to start at two and it was already one in the afternoon. He had to get moving, like right now, that memo would have to wait until tomorrow. After driving like a madman and finding a place to park at the stadium that was damn near in Ohio, he began running towards the gates where streams of loyal fans were waiting in line to get in.

Without realizing it, he damn near bumped into Ellie's car as he ran across an access lane outside the stadium. He was in line before she got her window down and shouted to him.

"Nash! Nash Gibson, over here!"

He looked in the direction of where his name was being called and saw her in the car. He stepped out of line and walked over to her car with a big smile on his face.

"Come on, get in. We can park on the other side and go in there," she said moving over in the back seat to give him room.

He opened the door and got in. As soon as he did, he could smell the subtle fragrance of her and his male senses were immediately heightened. He looked at what she was wearing and was glad he'd worn what he did. If people didn't know any better, they'd swear Nash and Ellie were married.

"By the looks of that line, you wouldn't have made it in till the first quarter was over."

"I know, I got busy at my place and let the time get away from me. In my haste, I forgot to call my friend and tell him I wouldn't be with him today. We have season tickets down in 'F' section in the fifth row." F section was on the forty-yard line and the fifth row would put them close to the Michigan player's benches.

"I could tell him," Jerome said from the front seat. Nash looked at the tall black man that was driving for the first time and wondered why he'd want to do that? "I'd rather sit in the stands than a box anyway. You feel the pulse of the game better that way." He was right, but Nash wasn't about to say anything. After all, this was a business meeting.

"You really don't mind doing this, Jerome?" Ellie asked.

"Shit no, boss lady. In fact, I'd prefer it."

Jerome parked the older model Cadillac Fleetwood limo that the company provided her in the box's parking area under the stands and they rode up to the box in an elevator, meanwhile Jerome headed for the stands. Nash was truly acting like a gentleman should and opened the doors for her like he'd been taught since childhood, then walked behind her down the hall to her box. After she used a key to unlock the box; he opened that door for her as well.

When he walked into the box he knew he was way out of his league by at least a margin of ten. Comfortable Michigan-Blue & Maze colored rocking type chairs faced the huge windowed wall overlooking the playing field. There were three rolls of six chairs each; the first row was down low and not more than two feet from the glass. The seats of the box hung over the stadium seats below it. Behind the rows of chairs was a wet bar stocked with all types of liquor's and beer, there was even beer on tap. They were the only ones in the box today and it seemed like such a waste to him, but these types of people didn't look at it like that.

"Would you like a drink before we take our seats," she asked, stepping behind the bar and putting her purse back there under the bar.

"A draft beer if it's not too much trouble," he said, standing at the bar watching her make herself a Bloody Mary. When she finished hers, she took a chilled mug out of the freezer and expertly drew a beer for him from a tap in front of her, one that didn't have too big of a head on it. He took both of their drinks down and placed them in holders next to the wall of glass. As she was coming down the four steps, he went back up to get his folder. She sat in one of the middle seats and he took the one on the edge, near the steps. He'd liked to have taken the seat right next to her, but he didn't think that was the right thing to do.

Looking down at the field, Michigan's Band was there playing a number while marching around making various shapes, however the sound came in through speakers over their heads and not directly from the field. The crowd was noisy too, but most of that noise was blocked out by the windows and the insulation of the box.

"It looks like we've got time now, so shall we get business out of the way before the game starts? I've got a bet on Michigan," she said easily and turned in her seat to face him.

"I'd like to bet on Michigan too, but I'm afraid Penn States a little too powerful for them this year."

For the next twenty minutes, they covered most of the questions and answers. Just before kickoff, she asked, "Nash, what's GM paying you?"

The question surprised him and it took a moment or two for him to answer.

"One seventy per, why?"

"Because I think you should come to work for me at Franklin and if you did you'd be heading up my new Development

Department. The first idea we could pitch would be this one. I agree with you that its potential is far too important to ignore. I'd be willing to put several million into developing a prototype and seeing if it really will work. If it doesn't, there are enough other aspects of this concept that will and we could incorporate them into some of our present systems."

"What sort of money and responsibility would I be looking at if I came to work at Franklin Industries?" he asked, looking at her intently to see if she was playing with him. She wasn't.

"VP in charge of Development and that position would bring two hundred and fifty per to start with. Interested?"

"Does that come with a full package?" He was asking if that included bonuses, medical, stock options and the rest.

"It does, but all ideas developed by you will be patented by Franklin. However, anything patented by your department would carry the name of the inventor and when it was developed, he or she would get a percentage of any royalties, let's say five percent blocks up to a total of twenty percent. That would be contingent on number of units sold and other considerations such as selling the rights to another firm," she said. She'd spoken the words to him, but what she was really doing was thinking out loud.

"Deal, boss lady, give me a few weeks to clean up my desk at GM and I'm your man," he said excitedly.

Ellie hit a switch and the windows of the box rolled back, instantly letting the full blast of the stadium noise enter the box. The game was an exciting one and the first half was an uphill battle for both teams. By the end of the half, Michigan was behind by three points. Ellie closed the glass and went up to the bar.

"What do you do for excitement, Nash? I know you've never been married and you aren't going steady with anyone either. Tell me a little about yourself?"

"How do you know I'm not married?" he asked, suddenly wary.

"I have my sources, but really, it's nothing more sinister than Charlie Anderson building you up. It was on his recommendation that you got the appointment yesterday. He'd talked to me about you over a month ago."

"That bonehead never said a word to me and I see him once or twice a month. Well, let me see, besides our annual bash up at the campgrounds I actually do like to camp out. Although not in a motor-home, I enjoy staying in a small tent that I pack in on my back and I stay in undeveloped areas that most tourists never get to see, that's because they are so remote and off the beaten paths that seldom get visited."

"Is that it?" she asked, watching him work his way through what he was going to say. She got the impression he'd only tell her what he wanted and that was it. He eluded privacy and was standoffish; she could detect that in his response because she did the same thing sometimes.

"No, I play softball in the summer and once in a while some of us old war-horses who played ball for Michigan get together for a keg of beer and to smash heads playing touch football, but the games always turn into full on tackle before the kegs gone."

"Does anyone get hurt?" she asked.

"Sometimes, but we're all so hard headed that it's only a broken finger or a nose. We're supposed to be tough enough to live with injuries like that so we play on."

"Are you that tough?"

"I've been lucky and only had bruises so far."

"You don't go out partying?"

"Not too often tho when we do it's usually as a group and we're in bed by ten. Most of the boys are married and being nearly forty years old, we tire easily."

"Yeah, I bet. How come you never married?"

"Is this my perspective boss or a very good-looking woman asking?" he asked.

"A woman. I put the boss's hat away an hour ago."

"Then to a beautiful woman I'd say, I've never meet anyone that I want to spend the rest of my life with. Because that's what it's going to be when I do get married, it's going to be for life. Ever since high school I always seem to look at a woman and try to picture in my mind what she's going to look and act like in forty or fifty years."

"Those are sort of some strange standards, aren't they?"

"To most, maybe, though not to me. Now then, let me ask you the same question? How come you never married?" he asked and looked into her eyes to see if she'd give him some standard answer or actually tell him the truth.

Looking just as directly back at him, she said, "I was more interested in my career than marriage. After beating my head against a male dominated wall, I used sex and my body to work my way to the top. But that was before. Now that I'm here, my bodies my own, no one else's."

The shock showed on his face, but his estimation of her went up several notches. She was brutally honest.

"You know that no matter what you do, you've got an uphill battle ahead of you?" he said meaning it in every sense of that statement.

"Don't I know it, but that's the reason I spend so much time staying on top of my profession. Let's stay away from business end of this meeting for the time being."

"Agreed. Any kids?" he asked.

"No, and I don't want any either. There are enough of them in this world and the pressure that's put on them is so great it's a wonder any of them grow up sane, and keep their narrow asses out of jail. What about you, do you have any little ones running around with your DNA in them?"

"God, I hope not. I don't think I'm daddy material. Oh, I could play ball with them, but when it came to doing the things like rising them right, I don't think I qualify."

The second half started and she opened the glass again. By the two-minute warning in the last quarter, Nash and Ellie were shouting along with the crowd. Michigan won by one point. They went to the bar and were on their second drink by the time Jerome got there and together the three of them went down to her car.

"Lady, would you like to have dinner with me tonight?" he asked, watching her climb into the back of the car.

She stuck her nose out from around the backdoor and said, "And what do you have in mind for afterwards?"

"A couple of times during the game I thought about some recreational screwing, but I've put those ideas away for the time being," he replied honestly, but he said what he did hoping to get a rise out of her, he watched the expression on her face. She wasn't surprised, nor was she put off. A smile was there instead. He continued with, "I thought diner at Ddeman Farms Restaurant out on Dancer Road would be in order and then we'd play it by ear from there. I've eaten their ribs and they're great, but if you don't want to go, I'll understand."

"It's time for you to be quiet and let me answer. I'll go for the ribs, but I have to be in early. I want to be up by seven in the morning and I don't want to be red eyed and tired."

"You got it, I'll pick you up at eight and promises to have you home by eleven; how's that?"

"Deal, and about that recreational screwing, don't put it too far on the back burner either, you never know when you might get lucky," she said, toying with him for a change.

"I won't, but by the same token I'm not holding my breath either."

She laughed and Jerome shut the door ending any further bantering between them.

Chapter Seven

The ride home for her was nice; that's because occasionally she liked playing the part of a normal girl and sparing with a fella was part of that, today happened to be one of those days. In addition to that he made her feel like a girl when she was with him. Opening doors, holding her elbow as she descended the steps, making a motion like he was standing up when she got up to make them another drink and letting her walk in front of him up the stairs, these were just some of the gentlemanly things he did. It was refreshing to see some old-fashioned manners being displayed these days.

Once, when he got up to use the private washroom that was part of the box, she'd openly checked out his butt and liked what she saw. He had an interesting face, rugged, yet surprisingly handsome. His sandy colored hair was just the right length and combed just so, thus telling her he was a little vane too.

He was honest, straightforward and not afraid to say what was on his mind. That crack about recreational screwing was very informational to her as well; she'd have to be careful with this one. He was out spoken and she got the impression that if she'd have asked him if he was any good in bed, he'd have told her. Then she realized what it was about him that she liked the most, he was a male version of her. If he was as tenacious about his career as he was about his private life, she knew she'd found a winner. He was, after all, going to be working for her and she'd have to weigh his attitude tonight in order to see if he let it influence his personal contact with her.

~♥~

On his way to find his car, Nash began kicking his ass for being so brazen with her because, after all, she was the woman who was, as of today, his new boss and was also going to invest some serious money into developing his pet project. So then, where'd he get off talking about screwing her? What a fucking idiot! But hey, wait a minute here, she only said she'd have dinner with him after he said what he did. Did she harbor the same thoughts?

He found his Jeep and managed to get on the road without being run over by one of the monstrous RV's, SUV's, or trucks that some of these people drove. Driving home, he continued his assessment of today's meeting and the possibilities of tonight's dinner. She rode in a limo and he drove a Jeep. However, he had an ace in the wings, for years he'd been restoring a 1934 Packard Roadster and had actually finished it last year. True, the car had spent most of its life under a tarp and taking up space in his garage, so maybe it was time to dust it off and see if it'd start. If it did, that was the ticket for tonight. To him, his car was ten times classier than that limo of hers. And what about taking her out for ribs? They were messy and they'd both have them all over themselves by the time they were finished, which brought him to another thought. He should wear dark clothing tonight.

Black turtleneck, sport coat and jeans were going to have to do.

~♥~

Ellie elected to wear a black dress. It was a dress that came down to just above her knees, nylons and high heels. And she fastened a diamond necklace around her neck, it hung down to just above her cleavage, it was as tho it were pointing the way to what lay below. She and Gina spent over two hours getting her hair and makeup just right, although Gina loved fussing over this vivacious boss of hers, sort of like a mother playing dolly with her daughter's looks.

Both women looked up at the gentle knock on her dressing room door. Jerome came in holding a ten spot out in front of him, waving it like a flag. He made no notice of Ellie's short robe, the one covering her nakedness, but he did comment on her hair.

"Nice job on the hair, only problem is that it's wasted on that jock, he won't notice," he said handing Ellie the money. "Next week UM's taking on Ohio State and I think I can get my money back. What do you say we bet twenty and I'll even give you three points?"

"You've got a bet. I think your wrong about the hair. That man misses very little and I'd go so far as say his hair will receive almost as much attention as mine is tonight."

"He's a jock and he'll expect you to fall all over yourself just being with him."

"No, that's what you did and it worked for a while, but now you have to work like a real man at getting laid and you don't like it. You can't judge everyone by your own pitfalls."

"Care to lay another twenty on it?" he asked, walking back to the door and turning to look at her.

"No, I won't bet on that, but I'll go you one better. If he's as vain as you say, I'll set you up with Della."

"What have I got to do if he isn't?" he said, interested. Della was a nice-looking mulatto secretary that worked for Bonnie in the outer office. He thought this was a sure thing and was prepared to back it up with whatever.

"If you lose, you drive me up to see my dad on Sunday and don't take any books to read. That way you'll have plenty of time to think about your feelings on your own."

"Deal! This is a win, win situation for me," he said, walking out the door and closing it behind him. They heard him whistling as he went down the stairs.

"What's this guy like?" Gina asked, pulling the robe from her boss.

Ellie picked up the thong panties and stepped into them, she damn sure didn't want a panty line tonight. For now, her unharnessed breasts swung freely as she moved about, so she stopped and looked at herself in the mirror. Before putting on her bra, she cupped them in her hands and asked Gina, "Do you think they're too big, for a woman my size I mean?"

"I think they're just right. God gave them to you and you should be proud of them. Put some body powder on them and a spot of perfume between them. You have the perfect shape and don't let anyone tell you different," Gina said, handing her the powder and putting the black demi-bra over her boss's shoulders.

The huge Packard purred sweetly as he drove down her street looking for the right address. He thought to himself, *she sure lives in a classy neighborhood*. The homes around here started at a cool ten mill, maybe more. Then another thought came to mind, maybe he should drive up to her house and honk the horn for her instead of getting out and going to the door. She was, after all, a woman and he had to forget the rest of that other shit for tonight and treat her like he would any other woman. But she wasn't just any other woman, she was, after all, Ellie, and she was his boss, it was going to be hard separating the two of them.

In the end he did both, he honked the cars horn, then jumped out and went to the front door and raised the massive doors knocker. Before he could drop it the door opened and there she stood looking like a million dollars and change. He was glad that he'd resisted the temptation to wear his jeans and had put on a nice pair of Hagar slacks instead, and then changed his shoes as well.

He let a soft whistle escape his lips as he stood there looking at her. "Lady, you look good enough to eat," then he stammered and said, "I didn't mean that to sound as crass as it did."

"I thank you for the compliment and I did take it in the context that you intended, relax." Looking over his shoulder she said, "That's some car you have out there mister."

"It's a 34 Packard Roadster. We can put the top down if you like, but it might get a little chilly if we do."

She stepped from the door, took his arm and said, "Let's leave it up for now." She'd spent too much time with her hair to have it messed up before the evening got started.

At the restaurant, he went around the car and opened the door for her, helped her out and stood tall. He was proud to have a woman as fine looking as Ellie hanging onto his arm. Once inside, the maître d' told them they had about a ten-minute wait and escorted them into the restaurants bar so they could wait there. They sat at the bar and ordered drinks, but before they were finished with them, the waiter came in to seat them and he took their drinks to the table for them.

They started out with a baked Asiago Cheese appetizer, followed by a Cobb salad. For entrées, Ellie ordered Seared Atlantic Salmon while Nash stuck with a New York Strip steak, medium rare. For dessert, she went for the Salted Carmel Cake, so he ordered a slice of Peanut Butter Pie and they shared.

During the meal they'd talked about ex-lovers, people they'd met on the job and people's kids. They both said they didn't want kids and then they didn't dig any further into that subject. In the car and headed home, Ellie said, "I'm not in that big of a hurry. Let's not end this evening yet."

It was after ten in the evening and Nash fell the same way, but they didn't want to go to some bar and drink either. Instead, he drove her to a spot he'd known about since high school, it's where he took his dates so they could watch the "submarine races", it was a make-out spot near the Ann Arbor Country Club. When they pulled in there were two other vehicles there, so he drove up a little way so they could be alone.

It wasn't that cool outside so they got out and walked down by the small lake. It'd been a long time, a really long time since Ellie was treated like this and it was refreshing to say the least. It made her feel young and beautiful; all of her cares were placed on hold. He even had a blanket for them to sit on near the water, which they did. She slipped her shoes off and she didn't know when or how it happened, but he ended up massaging her feet for her, it felt absolutely marvelous. As relaxed as she was, it was no surprise to her when she heard herself say, "Nash, will you make love to me tonight?"

With her shoes in her hand and the blanket over his shoulder, he carried her up to the car and placed her on the seat. He leaned in and kissed her full on the mouth, this was a passionate kiss complete with tongues and everything. While the kiss deepened, he ran his hand up her leg, but stopped just short of the Promised Land, although he did leave his hand resting on her inner thigh, it was very near a furnace that was burning on all cylinders. She reached out with her left hand and felt his hardness through his pants, he was more than ready.

When the kiss was over, he stood up. She didn't straighten her dress out, but he did try to alleviate some of the discomfort that was taking place in his pants.

~♥~

Nash parked his Packard at the front door and before he could get to it, the front door swung open and there stood Gina. "Good evening Gina," Ellie said, going through the door first. "We won't be needing you for the rest of the evening, thank you."

Like any good domestic servant, Gina promptly disappeared.

Nash was properly impressed with the grandeur of the house and his surroundings. What it told him was that he was way the hell out of his league with Ellie, but--? What was she doing with him, using him to scratch some itch she had or what? Women like Ellie could have her pick of the lot anytime she wanted, why him? Then it came to him, he was on the spot because he'd had enough nerve to actually ask her. He'd treated her like he treated all females, with respect and dignity, but like a woman, always like a woman. That she'd responded the way she was would always remain a mystery to him, but she had responded and here he was. He only hoped that this was not one of those one-night-stands, at least not the type that he himself had handed out so often.

She helped him over his nervousness by offering him a drink. They went into the dining room where there was a bar of sorts set up between two windows. He watched her move, it was really something to see. That black dress really worked on her. He felt himself stirring again so he looked about the house, he looked anywhere except where she was. They took their drinks into the massive living room and sat in front of the log-burning fireplace, a fireplace that was big enough to roast people like him in it.

After flipping a switch that ignited the gas burning fireplace, she sat next to him on the couch. Without saying a word, he took her in his arms and they repeated the sort of kiss they'd had in the car, only this time he didn't stop short, his hand found that furnace.

Moments later, they were on the rug in front of the fireplace; her legs were straddling his face, while her mouth was busy between his legs. Nash's tongue was working overtime on her nether lips, and he was finding what they hid. She was something else, every time he found what was hidden between those lips, she would have a mini climax. Twice he cried out in pain when she sunk her teeth into the tender flesh down there during one of her stronger climaxes, but she kept his manhood in her mouth and his testicles in her hand. His hands were busy too; they were working over her generous breasts, and he was moving his hands between them and her derrière. When he slipped a finger into her anus, she pushed her groin down so hard that she nearly smothered him.

Nash was like superman in that he was able to withhold his own climax, but it was difficult to say the least. Instead, he rolled her over, turned about and entered her womanhood using the missionary position. She grasped him to her with both arms and legs as he pumped himself into her. By exercising his manly strength, he pulled her to him, got on his knees without losing her or his connection with her, then stood up. He began walking about the room with her impaled on his manhood and it seemed like every step he took she climaxed, over and over, again and again. After two trips around the room, he laid her back down on the rug, rolled her over and pulled her hips toward him. She stopped him and instead pushed his hardness to her anus. He didn't need any further instructions, he pushed forward and sunk himself deep into her again. With him working her like he was, his hands were free, so with one of them he kept up the work he was doing on her breasts and the other he stuck between her legs and it took the place of his manhood, only now he could toy with both of the buttons that were hidden there. Twice, within a few moments, she screamed out in ecstasy, this also signaled to him that she was nearly finished.

He pulled himself from her anus and pushed himself into her other orifice, the one in front. This time she screamed loudly and fell face down on the rug while Nash emptied himself into her.

She felt the hot rush of his semen as it shot into her. Without thinking about it, she raised her backside up and backed into him so he could have even more access to her. Exhausted, he fell upon her and they both lay on the rug while his juices continued to flow out of him as his tool deflated.

She eventually rolled from under him and then snuggled into his strong arms. She stroked his face with her hand while he cupped her ass cheeks and held her to him. She kissed him twice, but they were not the barnburner kisses like they'd used before this latest tryst began.

"I could say WOW and mean it, but that would not come close to how you made me feel," she said, with a thick tongue and soft voice.

"I know, I felt the same thing. You really are quite some woman you know."

"You're not so bad yourself, buster. I think I had more real climaxes in the last hour than I've had in the past twenty years."

"So then, I guess that means that I'm going to stand a good chance of having a you agree to have second date with me then?"

"If it ends with something like this, absolutely, my pussy is going to be so sore that I doubt if I'll be able to pee out of it. And technically, this is our second date, the football game was our first."

"Is having a sore pussy a good or bad thing?" he asked toying with the erect nipple of her right breast.

"You've got to take your hands off me. I can't stand it anymore, you're driving me crazy. On the one hand I want more, but my body is telling me I've had enough. I'm so damn sensitive down there that I can feel the air between my legs."

"Then let me show you something that maybe you don't know about yourself."

He got up and went into the lavatory near the kitchen and came back with a glass of water, a damp towel and two dry ones. After rolling her onto her back, he pushed her legs apart and commenced cleaning her up. When she was clean down there, inside and out, he put one of the clean towels over her face so she couldn't see him.

Softly and ever so gently he put his face between her legs, pushed the thumb of his left hand into her anus and with his tongue working overtime, he went to work on her pubis, making sure he didn't go anywhere near her vulva or what it hid. When he found her clitoris, he sucked it into his mouth and using only his tongue began working it over. Soon her heels were beating a different tune on the rug, her legs were shaking and her tummy was convulsing, all involuntarily. Gasping for air, she sunk her fingers into his hair and pulled him up to her with the last ounce of strength left in her body.

With her watching him, he lifted his hand up to his face and began wiping away the juices that were coveting it and licking his hand clean.

"My God, you're an animal and am I ever glad you are. Now then, are you going to share that with me?" She pulled his hand to her face so she could smell and taste her juices as well.

Once they were back in each other's arms, she said, "I may have to take next week off to recuperate. I don't think I can move."

This time he stood up and picked her up into his arms. "Which way to your bedroom?"

She pointed and he carried her up the stairs, down the hall and into her suite. He headed straight for her bathroom. He sat her down on a cushioned chair by the vanity and with his manhood swinging in the breeze, he drew her a hot bath. He dumped some of this and that into it as the tub filled with water and the air became alive with the various fragrances. When it was just right, he picked her up again and this time gently placed her in the scented, hot water he'd put in the tub. She looked up at him and said, "Please join me, I don't want to do this alone. Not tonight."

She wiggled a little and made room for him as he got into the tub opposite her. After soaking and washing one another, twice to make sure they got everything, she stood up and he dried her with a warm towel from the holder next to the tub. She, in turn, reciprocated and then hand-in-hand they went to bed.

Her bed was big enough to be legally be classified as an aircraft carrier, but they found one another and soon she was snuggling up tight against his groin with her behind and he was holding her, one arm under her neck while his hand was cupping a breast. His other hand was busy touching the rest of her body, not sexually, but tenderly. The rest of the bed was unused that night; they could have slept on a singlewide bed for all the more room they took up.

Chapter Eight

It was Sunday morning and Nash didn't leave Ellie's house until after eleven-thirty and even then he was still exhausted. Ellie stood in the doorway watching him leave, never in her life had she been this sexually fulfilled and felt this content. Thank God, she'd had the presence of mind to call last night and canceled her appointment for this morning. There'd been many men in her life, but none could compare to Nash, he was in a class all by himself. Even while she stood there at the door, she could feel the tenderness of the flesh between her legs. Last night she'd been sore down there, like she had before, but this time it was worth it and this time it was a different kind of sore, this was a good sore. He was that great of a lover and he made her happy to be a woman. It's not that his manhood was overly large, it wasn't, but it was not small by any standards either. To her it was just the right in size and oh-my, how he could use that tool. She didn't think she was in love with this man, not yet anyway, but one could never tell anymore and she sure as hell liked him, that was more than evidenced by the way she was acting this morning.

After closing the door she headed back to her suite, she wanted to sit in the bathtub and soak away her aches and pains and to think. She was thirty-four years old, not some prom-queen out on her first date, so why was she so gaga over this man? But then why not, he was handsome, well put together, fun to be with, an outstanding lover, smart, ambitious, he had a great sense of humor and most of all he satisfied her every need or was that desire.

The water burned a little when it covered the tender flesh between her legs, but she opened them wide and let the magic of the scented water start to work. All her life men had sought out what she'd given to Nash last night, the difference was she had freely given herself, her sexuality wasn't taken from her or demanded or even required. Men had been using her body for their own gratification ever since she could remember. Last-night she'd used Nash's body to its fullest and was rewarded with how she felt today, absolutely wonderful.

Meanwhile, Nash drove home, took a quick shower and went to bed after setting his alarm for two hours. There were football games on today and he didn't want to miss any of them if he could help it. After his shower and while he was lying there in bed, Ellie came to mind. She was beyond beautiful, she was magnificent and she was quite the bed partner too. On top of that, she was smart, witty and could handle her own in any situation, well so far anyway. This was the type of woman who didn't need a man to make her life complete, she could manage her life's needs quite well on her own. Did he feel used, of course he did, but it was a good feeling this time. Sleep overtook him.

~♥~

They didn't see much of each other for the next two weeks, both of them were kept busy getting on with their lives, but they did talk on the phone a couple of times. The Monday morning that Nash walked into Franklin's offices, this time as an employee, he was directed to his new office, it already had his name on the glass door and there was a secretary seated in the outer office.

"Good morning, Mr. Gibson. My name is Alice Rich and I'm your interim secretary. Miss Masterson would like to see you at ten this morning in her office, that's the only appointment you have scheduled for now. Mr. Anderson would like you to call him when you have the time. Is there anything I can do for you at the present time?"

"Yes, Alice, fix us both a cup of coffee and come into my office. My name is Nash by the way. When you say Mr. Gibson, I start looking for my father. I take one sugar and a little splash of cream."

Once they had their coffees, Nash said, "Alice, I don't know what to expect here and I've never had my own secretary before, so if I'm not doing things right please correct me. I'm not much on protocol, nor am I much for routine. I sort of fly by the seat of my pants if you know what I mean."

"I do, sir and that won't be much of a problem, I'll adapt. Just remember that I'm a temp at best and I'm here to help you, but I'm not here to do it all either. Hopefully we can work together as a team."

"And I don't expect you to do it all. Believe me, we'll make this work. For now, get Charlie on the horn for me and then see if you can locate the projections for this quarter's output, I need to see the sort of numbers we'd need to carry my ideas to the next level. Next up, find me the information on any new inventions in the computer world that are listed on the internet, stuff that is pending, that sort of stuff. I don't expect to set the world afire, but I'd like to see what I'm working against so I can at least create some smoke. Hopefully the fire will come later."

After his conversation with Charlie, whereas Charlie wished him good luck, Nash got to work and before he knew it, it was time to go meet with Ellie. When he walked into her outer office, her secretary said, "Please go right in Mr. Gibson, Miss Masterson is expecting you."

When he saw Ellie, she was seated behind her desk and for a moment he wasn't sure if he should go over there and kiss her or what? He took the right path by saying "Good-morning, boss," and took a seat in front of her desk. No kiss.

She looked up at him smiling, and asked, "So did you get settled in?"

"Yes, my new secretary is a wiz. I like her. Can we make her my permanent secretary?"

"Mrs. Vandershot picked her out. I told her you'd need a fresh, yet intelligent, secretary that you could train to be yours. Talk to Mrs. Vandershot and she'll take care of that for you."

"Well she's that and more, thanks. So, what's up, boss?"

"In ten minutes, we are going in for a meeting with all of the department heads, I want to introduce you to them. After that, I want you to get together with some of them and give them the projected unit cost for your invention and then discuss the actual production of these units that you are proposing we develop. For now, I think you should build one and installed it in an existing car or truck so we could evaluate it. Afterwards we'll see about getting some of the automobile people in to see it. Then we can go from there."

"Agreed. I brought my schematics with me when I came in this morning."

"Good. Then the man you need to talk to is Henry Paterson, he's working for you now. Up until today he was in charge of the development of new products, but he's not an administrator or an idea man. He's a great nut and bolt man though, so use him, you won't be sorry."

Not once during this meeting or the one afterwards did Ellie even mention or give any hint that they had any sort of personal relationship and this sort of confused Nash a little. He knew she liked him so what type of game was she playing with him now? He was confused, but he did not let it affect his business sense or his job.

Ellie was right about one thing though, Henry was a virtual genius when it came to anything that was mechanical and electrical. They spent the afternoon going over Nash's idea and by the end of the day he had a much better idea about whether or not this was doable. For now it was a go, in Henry's estimation anyway.

"I can't believe that no one has come up with this idea before. It's so simple, maybe that's why. I've read about some other companies that have tried this, but the cost of building them far overrode them ever becoming practical. I'd wager we could produce these units for under five hundred dollars apiece once full production was started, then we could double that amount when we sold them to the auto manufactures," Henry said.

"So where do we go from here?" Nash asked.

"First thing in the morning I'll start laying out blueprints, on the computer of course and I think you should talk to Mr. Anderson in production and get his take on this."

"I don't think Mr. Anderson will be a problem, I've known him for a lot of years. We're old friends. But you're right, I'll schedule a meeting with him first thing in the morning."

Nash was still at his desk when Alice stuck her nose in the door and said, "I'm leaving now. Is there anything else you need before I leave?"

He looked at his watch; it was after five in the evening. The day had flown by, but he still had some other files to go over before he called it a day. "No, you have a good night, Alice. I'll see you in the a.m."

At six-thirty, he was still at his desk when suddenly his door opened and there stood Ellie. She walked in and stood before his desk, then asked, "Have you ever been laid in an office before?"

"No, and I don't plan on getting laid in this one either. What I would like is to take a beautiful woman out for supper and then take her home and screw her ears off. Does that sound like something you might be interested in?"

"It does. I already sent my chauffeur home, you're my ride."

"Can I look forward to this sort of thing to happen often?" he asked, as he drove them from the executive parking lot.

"Not if you don't want it to. It's up to you," she said, putting her hand on his leg.

"I do want it to happen and as often as possible."

Chapter Nine

It took every bit of two months of hard work and a lot of eighteen-hour days for Nash's idea to get off of the computer screen and become a reality. Franklin's engineers built his idea into a working project and then they got it installed into a Chrysler 300.

Now then, all they needed to do is find a test track where they could install all the proper road signs, they were the types of signs that were in use today, and then put the car through its paces. The computer they'd built for this test was big and bulky and it took up the entire trunk and back seat of the vehicle. Since there were so many checks and re-checks that had to be made and there was an enormous amount of redundancy built into this test unit too, that's why it took up so much space. In reality the finished product would easily fit onto the firewall of the car, it would be about the size of a small notebook computer. It would be both weatherproof and could stand the heat generated by the vehicles engine.

Using portable signs and going out only after dark, they set them up in Franklin's huge parking lot. They then placed a few obstacles in the way, used tape to lay out a road of sorts and then drove the car out onto the course. Nash was driving it that first time and when he flipped on the computer, he felt the computer take over the steering and other vehicle controls. He took his foot off the gas, removed his hands from the steering wheel and smiling from ear to ear he watched the car drive itself through the course. If the speed sign read 10, that's how fast the car went. It stopped at stop signs and yielded at crosswalks, but only if someone was standing there. When one of the developers stepped in front of the car, it swerved and applied the brakes, but did not stop and it didn't hit the pedestrian either. Next, two other cars pulled onto the course and the one directly in front of Nash slammed on his brakes, but the Chrysler stopped in time to avoid the impending collision. The car's new brain worked so well that Nash was tempted to get out from behind the wheel altogether, but he didn't. Instead, he came up with the idea of making the cars controls mostly imperatival once the new computer took over the driving skills for the human. When the small radar, a sound wave actuator and the other sensors that had been built into the car were working, the computer would and could react a hundred times faster than any human alive. On top of that the computer had been designed to learn, much the same way any new driver does and it would avoid any similar occurrences in the future, this was called a 'shared experience'.

But now then they had to get this contraption out on the open road and see if it would work in today's world. Out there, there would be a lot more for this computer to deal with than just road signs and a few other cars.

"What do you think? Is it ready for the supreme test, turning it lose in traffic?" Nash asked, unbuckling his seatbelt and exiting the car. That was one of the safety features, the computer would not engage unless the driver's seatbelt was fastened.

Another idea that had been tossed about during development, and that was installing a sensor that would keep the automobile from going over ten miles per hour if the sensor detected alcohol or if the driver was impaired in any way from any other substance. For now, they decided to leave it the way it was, but it was there for future development.

"I think so, but let's run this by the boss tomorrow before we do this. If something goes wrong, I want her to be aware of what we're doing," Henry said. Nash knew he was just covering his ass, but that wasn't a bad thing, it was the smart thing to do.

"Then put our baby away and make sure she's secure. I damn sure don't want anything to happen to our brain child, not now." Nash was both happy and proud that his idea had worked this good. It'd worked so well that if everything went accordingly, then in a few weeks they might be presenting this concept to the auto manufactures for their ideas and then begin to get their views on it.

Mattie was waiting for Ellie when she came in to work two days later. As Ellie passed her in Bobby's office, she thrust a copy of the Detroit Wheels News into her hand. "What's this?" Ellie asked as she opened the door to her office.

"It's a rag put out by a self-proclaimed public advocate. Look on the second page, there is a photo of a Chrysler 300 being driven in our own goddamn parking lot. The photograph is not very clear, but it did show a man reading something while the car was driving its self. The article goes on to explain that Chrysler officials were approached and they told this dickhead reporter that they know nothing about this. It also says that automotive automation will never work because there are too many variables out there in the real world, they could never make it as safe as a human driving is. Just read it and you'll see that we're mentioned all the way through this bullshit article."

Seated at her desk, with a fresh cup of coffee in hand, she began reading. It only took her about five minutes to read the entire article and if anyone believed this, then their new venture would be dead in the water before they even got started.

"Where in the hell did this bastard come up with our development cost and other numbers?" Ellie asked, tossing the paper across her desk in the direction of Mattie.

"I don't know, it has to be coming from someone inside. How far along are we with this project?" Mattie asked.

"We have a working test car now. Jay Marston's is busy locking up a racetrack in Canada, its location is supposed to be top secret. This weekend we're taking the car over there and putting it through its paces. If everything goes right, then you'll be task with getting the car people in to see a full-on test and they can inspect the car themselves at that time. At least that was the plan." Elli hit her intercom and said, "Bobby, get Gibson, Udall and Masters in here right away."

"Yes ma'am. Don't forget you have an eight thirty with Mr. Marsh of Victor Processors." Marsh was the CEO of Victor Processors; he was the supplier of most of the tiny semi-conductors that they used in the production of their computers. Tho he would just have to wait, this was far more important.

"Either cancel the meeting or find someone else to keep him busy until I'm finished with what I'm doing now. And get those three in here ASAP."

Ten minutes later they were all there and discussing the ramifications of this article. On the plus side, it wasn't a highly-circulated publication, but it was being circulated and that was enough to raise a red flag. The pebble had been dropped into the pond, now all they had to worry about was how big of a wave it would produce.

"Don, are we doing anything illegal by using that Chrysler?" Nash asked.

"No, once the vehicle is purchased, it's ours to do with as we see fit. Look at what those car racers do to the vehicles that they run at the tracks around this country. You've not altered the cars appearance in any way so I see no problems. But if you go into production with this hardware in the vehicle, then that's another story."

"And that's just it, these systems will only be available to the auto production industry, not the general public," Nash said.

Ellie looked at Mike Masters, VP of Security for Franklin and asked, "So how did this fool get close enough to get a photo like that in the first place and what do we do to prevent this in the future?"

"By the looks of the photo, it was taken with a high-powered lens meaning that they could have been a long way away when the photo was snapped. Since this was done in our parking lot and on a weekend, it is still accessible to the public. From now on, if you want these tests to be private then I suggest you bring our people into the loop so we can secure the site and keep things like this from happening again." He sounded pissed, but he really wasn't, just a little put out that he hadn't been in the loop to begin with.

"So, what do we do about this rag?" Ellie asked the three of them.

"Let me go over there and see what the hell he wants," Mike said.

"Alright, do that today and we'll have the rest of this meeting at five this afternoon. Jay should have our secure test site locked up for this weekend by then. I think you three should be there as well as Charlie Anderson and a few others. Let's keep the mechanics of this system secret as long as possible, no sense giving our competition a leg up on beating us out of the starting gate."

As the meeting was breaking up, Ellie asked Nash to stick around. "That's you in the photo, isn't it?"

"Yes, is that a problem?" he asked.

"No, but don't do it again. Hire a test driver, that way if anything goes wrong, well it'll be easier to explain that's all. Besides, I wouldn't like to see one of my VP's getting hurt doing shit like that."

"Why Ellie, you care."

"I care and let's leave it at that. And another thing, testing this car at this time of year may be a good selling point. If it can operate in inclement weather, like snow and stuff like that, then that would be a feather in our hat."

"Agreed, are you coming with us this weekend?"

"Absolutely, I wouldn't miss this for anything. It possibly represents the future of Franklin Industries. And besides I'd like to find time for you to visit me and put a smile on my face, I need one."

"Why Miss Ellie, that's the first time you've spoken about our affair here at the office. Now then, what does that mean?"

"It means that if you don't get your lazy ass out of here and get to work I'm going to fire you and replace you with a chimpanzee."

Nash got up, kissed Ellie on her cheek and left. She was smiling, but he didn't see that.

The test site wasn't at an airport like they expected; it was at a racetrack that was closed for the season and that made it even better, it was easier to control who saw what they were doing. The end of January was not exactly racing weather in Ontario, Canada. With the track as secure as Mike's people could make it, the test began at four in the afternoon. They wanted the test to run in both daylight and at night. As an added bonus, they had a mountain of snow that they could spread across the track for that part of the test, if need be.

It took a crew all morning and part of the afternoon to get the signs in place, and place the other obstacles where they needed to be. The test driver was a local racecar driver and he was looking forward to this job, he'd been out of work for the past several months and really needed the money.

The test started at four-thirty and for now the driver's helmet was outfitted with a special two-way radio that an outside scanner would not be able to pick up. For this test, all he had to do is flip the new computers switch on and then punch in the right coding for his destination. Since this was an oval one-mile track, they set up a monitoring station at both ends of the track for this part of the test as well as in the pits.

Once engaged, the computer put the car in gear, depressed the accelerator and they were off. Of course, all this was being recorded by a series of cameras that they had pre-positioned around the track and inside the car itself.

By the third lap around the track they were tossing obstacles in the way of the oncoming car and it was performing beautifully. With this part of the test satisfactorily under their belt, they switched the observation equipment that was monitoring the GPS part of the test car over to another facet of this test and placed five more cars on the track to act as traffic. While traveling at speed, the computer was turned on again and this time while it drove the car, the other cars would take turns cutting in front of it, stopping suddenly or slowing down without using their brakes and they would do anything else they could think of to confuse the computer. Like before, it performed flawlessly.

By this time of the day it was dark, so using what light they had they spread snow across the track in several places and again turned the car loose so it could do its thing. Once, when the snow was too thick in this part of the track the car slowed down and pulled over to the side of the track, and it did all this without any input from the driver.

Over the course of the next three hours they did everything they could to confuse the computer, but the more they messed with it, the better it preformed. They had a child test-dummy that they tossed out onto the track, in the snow, at night and the car detected it and avoided it.

This thing was more than ready for the public; they only hoped that the public was ready for it?

It was well after midnight when Nash and Ellie let themselves into her suite and Nash was exhausted. He'd tried to be in on every test they conducted to make sure his baby worked as planned. While he built them a drink, Ellie went into the bathroom and drew them a bath. She stripped down and when she came out, he was all eyes. Suddenly he wasn't as tired as he thought he was.

After a long and enjoyable, bath, Ellie dried him off and got him onto her bed, face down. For the next half-an-hour she worked over his tired muscles, but enough was enough and soon they were entwined with each other and this time she made him climax first. Later in the evening, after a short rest, he turned the tables on her and carried her into the stars for her climax fest.

With nothing more than a sheet over them, they fell asleep and didn't wake up until the phone rang the next morning at eight. They had breakfast in her suite, then joined the others at the track for some more testing.

As good as everything went yesterday, nothing went right today. The car ran red lights, couldn't stay on the road on its own, it was like the computer wasn't hooked up at all. That meant it was time for the mechanics to go to work, what else could they do.

Mike and Nash had their noses in on everything the mechanics did while Ellie and the others went to a nice restaurant to await the outcome and to see what had gone wrong. It took a while, but they eventually found where three wires had been cut, then spliced together, but without actually making contact. This was not an equipment failure; this was pure and simple sabotage.

Nash turned to Henry and said, "Didn't you have guards on the car all night?"

"Yes, we put it under a cover and I had two men here all night."

"Get hold of them, I want to talk to them," Nash said, he was more than pissed now.

While Mike called his men, Nash watched them replace the wires. This was getting serious now. This was going beyond some idiot writing a bad report on their project.

The four men whose job it was to guard the car overnight stood there in front of Nash. "Can any one of you tell me if anybody was near the car last night?"

They shook their heads negatively and looked at each other.

"Well someone got to it and it was your responsibility to protect it. Now what do you have to say about that?"

Knowing that talking to them this way would get him nowhere, he went to his rental car and took one of the guards with him. One on one, he went through his questions and still came away with nothing, they all answered the questions about the same. "What did you do if one of you had to use the restroom?" he asked the third one.

"We stayed right there and pissed on the ground, we never left that car."

"Did either of you go to sleep?"

"Nope, we were there talking for our entire shift, I like Billy, we have a lot in common."

"While you were talking, where were you in relationship to the car?"

"We had two chairs sit up about eight feet away and that's where we spent most of the night. We drank coffee and could see around the entire area."

"Were you in front of the car or off to the side?"

"Kind of to the front, though off to one side, the driver's side."

"Was the car locked when you guys put the tarp on it?"

"No, I don't think it was. You guys took the keys when you left, that's the way you lock its doors, you do it by using the fob."

That explained it, they were all telling the truth. While they were busy talking and drinking coffee, someone had snuck up to the car, crawled under the tarp and had gotten inside. Once in there, they cut the wires and reattached them in such a way that they'd made the computer completely useless.

Nash got out of the rental and shouted to the repairmen. "Make sure you keep those wires, I want them when you're finished."

After the four men left, Nash called Mike over and said, "It wasn't those men's fault, it was ours. They did their job to the standards we left with them. Never in a million years would I have thought someone would be so dead-set against our project working. Get this through your heads, from this point forward I want that car to be under lock and key and be guarded at all times or I'm going to skin someone alive."

Once the car was working as it had yesterday, Nash sat down and looked closer at those wires. Where the breaks were, there was a small cut made so a tool could be inserted inside the insulation to cut the wire. Then the wires were pulled a little, giving separation to the wires. The only way they found the breaks was by running a continuity test on each and every wire. Maybe if they made this a plug-in unit and keep the wires together like in a wire-loom, or actually had the wires made in specific groupings, that was the ticket. So, some good was coming out of this delay after all.

While all this was going on, Ellie was seated in the stands with Mattie and Mattie was ecstatic about how this computer was doing its job thus far. Yesterday she'd watched the test and couldn't wait to get behind the wheel of this car and see how it felt to be driven by a machine.

"Are you going to let me get behind the wheel? Please." Mattie asked.

"We'll see how things go now that it's working again. However, I don't see any reason we can't all have a go at this concept car today. I'll talk to Nash and see what he thinks."

But in the end Ellie didn't get behind the wheel or even in the test car, she was busy with other things, there was still an active, working, company to run and she was the CEO.

Chapter Ten

Fray Bennington was ecstatic that his little plan was working as well as it was. If Ellie fell on her ass and ended up spending this much cash on something that didn't work, then he would have an excuse to point the finger at her and possibly get her not only fired, but arrested. He'd never been fired in his life and he didn't like it, not one bit. Thank God, he still had a few friends left that was still employed with Franklin.

Thus far his little crusade against Ellie was working perfectly and up until this point it'd only cost him a little over two hundred grand. It wasn't like he didn't have the funds, he did and then some. With nearly four hundred million to play with, money he'd fleeced from the company in the first place over the years, he was well funded. Now then all he had to do is keep it hidden from his goddamn no-good moneygrubbing wife.

He would have liked to have seen their faces when that car didn't work the way it should have in Canada. He'd have to thank Jay Marston's and to some extent Charlie Anderson when he saw them again. But he didn't leave things where they were, he had to keep the pressure on them and what better way than the real press. He still had a few contacts left in the automotive world too, contacts that would love a juicy story like this.

"Pat, this is Fray. Would you like to have dinner with me at my place tonight, I think I may have a story for you." Patrick Murphy was a reporter for the Detroit Free Press.

~♥~

Meanwhile, Mattie and her bunch were busy cutting and splicing together a dynamic video presentation, one that would highlight this new Franklin development and she had to get this done before the Super Bowl add submission deadline, that gave her about six days.

On top of managing this madhouse, Ellie had other problems to deal with, one of them was the up and coming union contract with the rank and file, another was a shipping problem, meaning that life went on in-spite of this project of Nash's. All day Monday and part of Tuesday was taken up with the shipping dilemma, with a few union reps thrown in here and there from time to time for good measure.

Like most companies did these days, they didn't keep a large inventory of spare parts or for that matter any parts they didn't produce themselves on hand. They would simply order in a shipment of parts to arrive at a specific time, usually the day before they would be used or needed. However, here of late these parts were arriving late, thus causing her to have to slow production down to accommodate both the suppliers and the shippers and this was costing her money in the long run.

One of these items were specific-duty microprocessors, they were being shipped in from a factory in St. Louis, Missouri. Usually they came by truck, but here of late Franklin had been forced to have the shipments come in by air in order to get them there on time, thus causing the shipping cost to become unsustainable.

This prompted her to fly to St. Louis so she could set down with the CEO of Morris Semiconductors, one on one. She'd met

Ralph Morris twice before, he owned the company and was a great nuts and bolts man, however he was no administrator. Perhaps that's why he hired others to run the company and leave him with the production side of it. At any rate, she was meeting with him today.

"Ralph, it's good to see you again," Ellie beamed as she walked into his office. She was dressed in a severe business ensemble, but anyone with a lick of sense could see there was a beautiful woman hidden away in there.

After the niceties were over, Ellie got right down to the real reason she was there. "Ralph, someone is deliberately delaying shipments to us and it's hurting our production. For the past month we've had to resort to having the processors shipped in by air, but that's damn expensive. I'm going to tell you right up front that if we can't get this fixed today, right now in fact, I'm going shopping for a new provider. I know it sounds sort of harsh, but I have a business to run too."

"And we wouldn't like to lose your business either. I know for a fact that Fray Bennington called our shipping office and told them that no matter what your people said at Franklin, that the shipments were coming in way too fast. He said that you people didn't have enough room to store that much product and for us to delay sending any further shipments for one week beyond what the order called for. I know about the air shipments, but I figured it was just to cover specific shortages you were experiencing on the short term."

"Ralph, Fray Bennington was fired from Franklin over three months ago, I fired him myself. Why he's sticking his nose into our affairs now is anyone's guess, but if you can get the shipments fixed then I'll handle Fray myself. On another subject, we are developing a new system that would probably use four of your new processors per unit. If this goes the way I think it will, we may be doubling or tripling our requirements soon. Can you handle that much product?"

"Not a problem. In fact, we'll open up a line specifically for your product."

"How long would it take you to get set up to do this?" she asked.

"We already have the room. I'd say a week, is that fast enough?"

"It is and thank you. I knew coming here and talking to you direct would fix this."

While she was in the rent-a-limo and on her way back to the airport, she called Nash.

"I have a name for our nemesis, its Fray Bennington. He's the man I ousted when I took over as CEO. Get hold of Mike Masters and Don Udall and tell them I want to see them, along with you, before you guys call it a night. I'll be back to town in about two hours, set the meeting up for five in the small conference room."

But after a tie-up at Lambert-St Louis International Airport, the meeting was set back an hour, they were late lifting off the runway do to a bomb scare at the airport. All flights were canceled or delayed until the bomb squad cleared them. Then her jet was put in a holding pattern at Willow Run Airport, it was between Ann Arbor and Detroit. Apparently, a cargo plane had gotten too close to the side of the runway and one of its wheels broke through the frozen ground and the aircraft ended up getting stuck. They had heavy equipment out there trying to remove it, but in the meantime the jets wing was blocking the runway. This took another two hours so Elli rescheduled the meeting for nine the next day.

Five minutes later she called Nash again, "Hey you, do you feel like having a late supper with me and then maybe we could do a little of that stress relief stuff that you do so well?"

"Sounds like a plan lady. I'll meet you at your house."

"No, wait for me at the plant. I want to eat out and then we can go to your place for a change."

"I'll be here. Besides I have things to do here at the office so that'll work out great for me. See you when you get here."

It was close to eight when Ellie came waltzing in and she was carrying two sandwiches and drinks from a "Subway" franchise. "Let's eat here and then I want you to make love to me. I need to forget the pressures of this job for a few hours and you're just the ticket for that. You game?"

"Lady, I was born game."

While Nash cleared his desk off so they could use it as a table, Elli slipped out of her business suit and sat down wearing nothing except her lingerie. Not wanting to feel over dress, Nash did the same thing.

Halfway through the sandwiches, Nash once more cleared the desk. He tossed their clothing on the desk, picked Ellie up and laid her on the desk. Slowly and deliberately he finished undressing her, then himself. While she wreathed around on the desk trying to watch him undress, he told her, "Lay still or I'm going to spank you."

"That sounds like fun too, but not tonight. I really need you."

He positioned his office chair at the end of the desk, sat down on it and pulled Ellie over to the edge so that her legs were draped over his shoulders.

"What sort of devilment to you have in that complicated head of yours?" she asked, raising her head up to look at him.

"Just relax, I'm sure you'll like it whatever it is."

And she did too. After running his hands over her, he lowered his face to her vagina then used his tongue to open her nether lips before sucking her clitoris into his mouth. While his mouth was busy, he inserted his finger into her and sought out her "G" spot. With both of her buttons being stimulated at the same time, she began to orgasm and for a full ten minutes he kept after her until she was experiencing one organism after the other, uncontrollably. Some were so strong that for a second or two she'd black out, then come around shaking and screaming in ecstasy. When he stopped, she fell back onto the desktop completely exhausted, she was nothing more than a bowl of Jell-O in warm quivering skin.

He stood up, leaned over and kissed her, but she was almost unresponsive. Never in her life had she been this completely satisfied. She felt used, but it was a good feeling, not a bad one.

As feeling came roaring back to her groin, she could feel his hardness pressing against her. Somehow, she got her hand to move and she reached down between them, grasp his pulsating hardness and pushed it into her soaking wet canal. No other effort was needed on her part, he took over and as he built toward a release himself, she felt herself rise to the occasion one more time. Their love juices flowed together and flooded her receptacle to overflowing. She could feel their lives forces flowing down across her buttocks, between her cheeks. Suddenly, she remembered she was lying on their clothing and put her hand down there to keep it from staining their things, but it was too late for that.

He stood up and she rolled off the desk so no more fluid would leak from her. She ran over to his lavatory and went inside. When she came out, he was still sitting there where she'd left him. She walked over and sat on the desk facing him.

"I'm going to have to keep this little session in mind. The next time I'm feeling all stressed out I'm going to bring you in for a private meeting. Right now, I am so wasted that I can hardly walk; I'm weak as a kitten. You promised to tell me someday where you learned how to do that to a woman."

"And I will, someday, but I think we should be lying in bed with our arms around each other when I do this." He reached for his underwear while she began to get dressed too.

Before he opened the door so they could leave, she stopped him, put her arms around his neck and kissed him hard. He reciprocated and when the kiss was over she said, "Mister, I think I'm falling in love with you."

"That's good, because I have been in love with you for a couple of months now."

"When did you know for sure?" she asked.

"I think it was shortly after coming to work here at Franklin. When I didn't see you every day, my heart hurt like the dickens and I missed you more than breathing or eating. The weekends we didn't get together were the hardest I think."

"That's probably the nicest thing anyone's ever said to me. I love you too."

He opened the door and they left hand in hand like a couple of teenyboppers.

Chapter Eleven

At the meeting the next morning there was an extra person in the room, she was a longtime friend of Nash's. Regina Williams was a handsome looking woman, but there would be no mistaking her for beautiful. She was somewhat of a muscular built person, pretty in the face, but her mannerisms and overall build were those of a man. She was brisk, outspoken, tuff as nails and black as midnight. When the others were introduced to her, she shook their hands like a man and was as strong as one too.

She and Nash had met when they were both in the eight-grade and at that time, he'd befriended her when some white boys were hazing her for coming out for boy's football. The following day she'd dropped out of the sport, but she and Nash remained good friends. After high school and two years of college, she took a job as a secretary for a private investigator. Less than a year later, she took the test and was now a licensed PI herself. Three years after that she opened her own business and by spending ten successful years in business, she now was the boss of four other licensed PI's and had an overall staff of ten working for her. RW Investigations was the name of her firm and she'd just recently opened an office in Toledo, Ohio and another in Lansing.

"I brought Regina in on this because I have a feeling we're going to need a pro to get to the bottom of this. For the present time and given the circumstances, I don't think it's time to bring in the cops. That's because I think that Regina can do what they do, only better. She's fully licensed and accredited in the state of Michigan, Ohio, and Indiana. As of this morning she is working for us so be as free and open in front of her as necessary," Nash said, after introductions.

Ellie and Regina hit it off right from the start, probably because they were women in charge of men, but whatever the reason was they instantly liked each other.

"So, what are we going to do about this prick?" Mike asked. His job was security, he was not hired to be a cop. He was glad that Regina had been called in; it took the pressure off him.

After they talked for a few minutes, Regina said, "Folks, Nash sort of filled me in on you-all's problem earlier this morning. If this Bennington fellow thinks he's being smart, I'm here to tell you he's not. I'm going to turn my gang loose on him and we'll nail down the extent of his involvement in this seemingly breach of ethical codes. If he's broken the law, we will bring in the authorities and then turn all of our findings over to them. What we need from you is for you to go about your business as if nothing was going on, we'll take it from here on out. Oh yes, one other thing, we are going to need full access to all of Franklin Industries facilities, can that be arranged?"

It was and the meeting was over in five minutes. When Ellie, Nash and Regina went into Ellie's office, the talk was not about business, the two women started becoming friends and they really did have a lot in common, and that common thread was Nash. Although Nash had never been with Regina sexually, she had a treasure trove of personal information about him that she openly and freely was willing to share with Ellie. After one cup of coffee with them, Nash wisely retreated to his own office and left them alone.

"How'd you two ever become friends?" Ellie asked.

"At the start of the eight-grade I decided I wanted to play football. Since the school didn't have much of a girl's athletic organization, I joined the boys team, much to the chagrin of the others on the team. Four or five of the boys were giving me a hard time when Nash walked over, pushed his way in front of me and it was evident none of those boys wanted to tangle with him, so they left me alone. After practice, Nash walked me home and then he sat on the porch with me for a good hour or two explaining why those boys were reacting like they did. Even though most of what he was saying was pure horseshit, I quit the team the next day. After that Nash and I spent a lot of time together as friends, close friends. That man doesn't have a bigoted bone in his body, he never once looked at my color, he only saw me as a friend. Even when he played college football, he and I remained close friends, he even got me a pass for all the home games that were played in the 'Big House'. Once or twice, we went out for drinks, but we were never lovers. This was not something that ever came up between us, we are friends and that's the end of that. I knew if I ever needed his help, he'd be there for me and he knew I'd be there for him if he needed me. Maybe that's why I crawled my lazy ass out of bed at five this morning to have breakfast with him while he clued me in on what was going on and then asked me if I could help. I can you know, but it may take a little time."

"There's the crutch of it, we don't have the time. We need to nip this in the bud right away, before any more damage is done, damage that we can't repair or cover up. A lot of our business with the automakers is perception and if we lose our credibility with them, then we're out of business altogether. Take a look at what happened between Firestone and Ford and you'll have some idea of that perception thing."

"Then I guess I'd better get my ass moving. We'll give you a written bi-weekly report on our progress, but if we come up with anything hard we'll notify you right away."

Before Regina could leave Ellie's office, Nash came in with a Detroit Free Press newspaper and plopped it on the desk between the two women. "Now someone has really done it. Take a look at that shit," he demanded angrily as he pointed to a story in the paper.

Franklin Industries is at the heart of a project that would take the human driver out of the driving equation and turn the driving skills over to a machine. This reporter has been a driver for more years than he'd like to admit to, but there is no way a machine can ever take the place of a human behind the wheel of an auto. That might be fine for a drone that flies in the sky; there is no real traffic up there, not like there is on the Edsel Ford Expressway at five in the afternoon.

The story went on for a few columns, but the grist of his story was an open attempt to kill their new project. Regina looked at the both of them and said, "We're on it," and left.

Two days later that same reporter had another article in the newspaper, this time its headline was, "How to Sleep your way to the Top." Two columns were devoted to chronologically listing the life of an unknown woman who worked for a computer company located in Ann Arbor, one that had strong ties with the automotive industry. No names were mentioned, but it mirrored Ellie's rise to the CEO's chair almost as closely as if the reporter had read her diary, that is if she was stupid enough to keep one. It did everything except directly name her.

If they thought they'd pissed her off before, they had no idea what this article did to Ellie, she was livid. Not that most of what was printed wasn't true, it was, but to see in print right there in front of her and for all to see, it enraged her. Then her brain kicked in and she realized that this could have only come from one source, that fucking Bennington. If he had been there at this very moment she'd have ripped his goddamn head off and shit down his neck. She grabbed for her cell phone.

"Hi, you busy?" she asked, when Nash answered his phone.

"Yes and no, what's up boss?"

"Would you please come to my office?"

"Sure, I'll be there in five."

After he read the article, he looked at Ellie and laughed, she was red faced and still pissed. "Relax, the only people who are going to know who this is either works for or did work for, Franklin. Besides all that is in the past, its ancient history. I happen to know that you haven't given a blow job to anyone except me for over three months."

"And how do you know that, mister smart ass," but she was smiling for a change.

"Because anyone who gets a blow job from you is going to have a smile on his face for at least a day or two and I haven't seen anyone who fits that category." He paused for a second before saying, "Anyone except me that is."

"Get over here and hold me. You are good medicine for me. Thank you."

While she was in his arms, her intercom came to life. "Miss Ellie, Mrs. Sanders is here to see you."

"Send her in and thank you."

When Mattie came in, she went directly to the TV and put a DVD into the player and then sat down. "Come on you two, you might like to see what we've done with this."

The DVD ran for about ten minutes and it showed most of the staff that had driven the Chrysler during its test in Canada. It highlighted what the car could do from both outside and inside the vehicles prospective, how it reacted to various scenarios and especially how it handled problems. All this was done complete with narration and music, it was masterfully done.

"When do I get a copy of this?" Elli asked.

"This one is yours," whereas she produced another and gave it to Nash. Then she pulled another disk from her bag of tricks and put it in the player. This one held a one-minute commercial, along with a thirty-second one and another that ran for ten seconds. She'd really been busy and the commercials were perfect, they showed this project in a really good light.

"Mattie, can you get this on the national networks right away, even before the Super Bowl?" Elli asked.

"Sure, all it takes is money. When would you like this to run, I mean what time of the day or night?"

"Let's shoot for two spots, one during the evening newscast and another between eight and eight-thirty weeknights. What is something like that going to cost?"

"Usually a minute of the newscast runs about three hundred thou, the eight to eight-thirty timeframe is higher, usually about a half million for a minute."

"Wait a second here. Don't we have some time during the Super Bowl?" Nash asked.

"We sure do, do you want to use this on them?" Mattie asked.

"Yup, and then for a week afterwards run it twice for the six o'clock newscast, let's say Tuesday and Thursday, and once on the later timeframe, you chose the day that's the best."

"Okay, but you can plan on Bart screaming bloody murder," Mattie said.

Bart was their finance guru, he usually complained about the cost of ink pens and this was sure to tip him off the deep end. Nevertheless, these ads were going to be run so he'd just have to learn how to live with it, sort of how he learned to accept the cost of shipping the parts they needed by air.

When Mattie departed, Nash kissed Ellie and he too walked out the door, he had work to do. Sitting there at her desk, Elli suddenly she felt so alone. Being the boss wasn't all it was cracked up to be, it was trying at best and downright madding at times. She shook her head, signaled for Bobby to come in and got back to work herself.

~♥~

Seemingly, Fray was scoring at will these days and with no repercussions. He thought he'd covered his back trail so nothing would lead to him, but he was wrong. Regina and another PI that worked for her, a white man named Billy, was hard on his ass. While Regina was at the Free Press, Billy went to St. Louis to get a written statement from the CEO of Morris Semiconductors, Ralph Morris. He was only too happy to give them one, he wanted to keep doing business with Franklin Industries.

Meanwhile, back in Michigan, Regina wasn't having that much luck. The editor would not allow her access to the newsroom, so she had to wait for the reporter to leave the building before she could confront him.

Patrick Murphy came out around seven that night and when he did, Regina didn't approach him, she followed him and yes, she was that good. He went home; he had a house in Ferndale. When he went into the house she waited until nine before knocking on the door.

Flushed with his supper and seemingly happy with his life, Regina rained on his parade when she told him that some of what he'd published in that first article was confidential information obtainable only by industrial theft and that made him liable. He tried to bull his way through that shit, but Regina wasn't having any of that, she stood her ground and in the end he gave up his source, it was no sweat off his nose at this point.

But even with his confession it wasn't enough to hang Bennington, not in a court of law anyway. Although she did have something and it was something more than she had going into this investigation. Perhaps she could use it in another way, a way that would make everyone happy.

Chapter Twelve

The jet's pilot sat them down softly on the runway and it rolled to a stop at the terminal. As soon as they could, the two lovers, Nash and Elli, deplaned and headed for luggage area. It was nearing ten at night but nothing could dampen their spirits, not even darkness. They were on the island of Jamaica and headed for a private resort called "The Caves", who wouldn't be happy. This was supposed to be a romantic weekend for them, they both needed to get away from the pressures of Franklin Industries for a while and they knew if they stayed in town, work would follow them.

Even though it was late when they finally went to sleep, Nash was up early. He ended up having to prod Ellie and coherse her into getting up with him in order to take a run on the beach, then he wanted her to swim out to a tiny island with him, it was one that they could see from their cabin.

"I'm still tired. Where in the hell are you getting all this damn energy, you taking drugs to keep you going?" she moaned, as she staggered into the bathroom and sat on the throne.

"Yes, I'm taking a very addictive drug, it's called Ellie's Ecstasies, and just the smell of her moves me to do superhuman feats. Now get that lazy ass of yours moving or I'm going to pick that sexy ass up and toss it in the ocean and then hold your head underwater. Now, get a move on, we're burring daylight."

"I'm going to burn something and it's not going to be daylight." But she finished her business and headed for the bedroom.

Dressed in swim suits, ten minutes later they were running up the beach barefoot. After a twenty-minute run, he had them both in the water swimming towards that speck of an island. Twice they had to stop to catch their breaths, but they swam the quarter mile or so to the island in good order. This island had somewhat of a beach, but it was evident that not many people visited it.

Being alone, Nash stripped off his suit and began helping Elli out of hers. "My God, but you are a beautiful woman. Most women look better with clothes on, but not you, you're even sexier with them off. Maybe we should become nudist, that way I could show you off properly. I love you, lady."

"Well, I'm not becoming a freaking nudist so forget that shit. Let's just lay here on the beach and take a nap."

They did just that, but every ten minutes Nash had her awake so she could turn over so she wouldn't get sun burnt. After thirty minutes of the sun he was ready to head back. When they went to put their suits on again they were dry, the sun had worked its magic.

It took them a little longer to swim back, Elli was more tired that even she expected to be. When they got to the beach in front of their cabin, she lay there and said, "I'm not moving for the next hour, and if you come near me I'm going to castrate you."

He ignored her threat and scooped her up in his arms and carried her up to the cabin. Once inside, he pealed her wet suit from her luscious body and stood her up in the shower. After a quick rinse-off, she was in bed with the sheet pulled up to her neck. "Don't you want to eat breakfast?" he asked.

"Leave me alone. You can wake me up for supper and not before."

Nash took a shower and crawled into bed with her and they both slept until noon. After dressing and in much better sprits, they went up to the main resort and ate a hearty-man's lunch and then they went sightseeing.

~♥~

Meanwhile, in Michigan and fighting six inches of snow, Regina and her little band of pirates were busy. Fray already had his own shadow; if he left the house, it was being documented where he went and who he saw or talked to. Regina sent another of her troupe after the editor of that rag, the one that had nothing except negative things to say about the new Franklin Project. Since it was the weekend, this operative was given the okay to break into the reporter's house, if necessary, which he promptly did.

Arthur Sand's house was out of town, just off of West Liberty Road, and he found a treasure trove of information in the man's den. Rather than simply steal it, he fired up this fool's printer/copier and ran off copies of everything he found. During his search of the house, he discovered a recording that had been made with a small cassette recorder. This was low tech for sure, but there were two cassette tapes in this cup on a high shelf in the kitchen.

It took some doing, but he eventually found the recorder, put one of the tapes in it and found that he had a recording of Fray Bennington talking with this slime-ball. The other tape was of a woman and him discussing something about a Ford project. After listening to them again, he now had a recording of them on his Blackberry phone. Then it was time to put everything back where he found them, no sense tipping his hand yet.

Then he hit the jackpot, the computer hadn't been turned off, it was in a sleep mode, all he had to do is move the mouse and it was on. From it, he came away with bank statements and e-mails that had been sent back and forth between Arthur and other people in the auto business. After using nearly a ream of paper copping most of this stuff to hardcopy, he pack up, picked up and disappeared.

That evening, at Regina's office, they were busy going over all the shit her man had come away with. Some of this stuff was dynamite, but not all of it was directed towards Franklin Industries. Most of it was intended to be used against the big three, Ford, GM, and Chrysler. Talk about coming away with a bargaining chip, they had one now, a big one. Where in the hell did this nobody come up with all this information and why? He had to be a stickler for paperwork; there were tons of it in Regina's estimation.

"I want you to go through Bennington's place like this. Think you could do it?" she asked her man, Vic.

"Piece of cake. He still goes to church with what's left of his family on Sunday's, right?"

"He does. And to be on the safe side we'll set up a blocking force in case they come home early and you're not finished. Do you need any help?"

"I'll take Judy with me; she can help me cart the shit out when I'm finished."

Judy was another of Regina's staff; she'd been with her for two years. Regina had picked her up directly from the Michigan State Prison for Women and she'd been with her ever since being released from custody. She'd been convicted of breaking and entering, grand larceny, (she'd stolen two hundred grand by using the mark's own computer), and two counts of fraud. She had served only four years of a seven-year sentence; in fact, Regina had been her parole officer for a time. This young woman was all skin and bones, tall, but highly skilled with the computer and she acted more like a cat-woman when it came time to do the actual dirty work.

~♥~

When Ellie got to the office Monday morning, there was a note on her desk stating that Regina wanted to see her and Nash sometime today and that it was important. Hitting her intercom, she said, "Bobby, call Regina and ask her to come in around noon. Then inform the kitchen staff that we will be having lunch in the executive dining room at twelve-thirty. Tell them that there will be five for the businessman's lunch. Then contact Mr. Gibson's office and tell him to come to my office around noon."

A businessman's lunch to Ellie was a hot roast beef sandwich, fries, coleslaw, a glass of tomato juice and of course the ever-present pot of coffee. The food notwithstanding, most of the time the executives went out for lunch, that way they could have a mixed drink or two without anyone looking over their shoulders. One of their favorite places to eat was Paesano's Restaurant; it was right on the main drag, Business US-23. In fact, this was where Ellie had met the old Chairman of the Board the day she screwed him until he died, but not before he gave her everything she'd ever want and then some.

At five after twelve and once everyone was in place and settled down, Regina asked, "How deep do you want to go in this investigation?"

"We want the negative shit about our product to stop and we don't care how it's done at this point," Nash said.

Regina's next question surprised them all. "Can everyone in this room be trusted?"

This time it was Ellie who spoke up, but not before the four of them looked at one another strangely. Ellie knew for sure that she could trust Nash, that went without saying, but what did she know about Mike Masters or Henry Paterson, not much, but she was willing to go out on a limb and vouch for them. "I think we can trust everyone here, why?"

"Because you have a mole, someone who is feeding information to the outside and it's gone way beyond the boundaries of Detroit, it's worldwide."

"Then let's take this one step at a time. What did you come up with on Fray Bennington?"

Regina shuffled a few papers, looked at the one she sought for a moment, then said, "He is sort of the instigator of this original problem, but it's gone way beyond him now. He's the one who contacted the mole here at Franklin and before you ask the question, let me answer it, we don't know who it is that is feeding them the information, yet. Anyway, it was Bennington who contacted Arthur at that publication and put him on the case, for a fee that is. Arthur charged Bennington one hundred grand for his involvement in this, but there again the moles name never came up, yet it was his, or their, information that was used, not Fray's or Arthur's. Bennington then contacted Jay Marston in Canada and we are still trying to lock that down, but we have reason to believe that Marston is the one who hired a professional to sabotage your car that weekend. Hopefully, by the end of the Super Bowl this weekend, we'll have this professional's name and the full extent of Jay's involvement."

"Something tells me that there's more. Please continue so we can get the full picture," Ellie prompted.

"Somehow, I don't know how, your mole has been in contact with Mercedes. Not the U.S. company, but directly with Germany and we believe this was through Fray Bennington, he's the go-between for now. Apparently, Mercedes has been working on something similar to what you've developed, however theirs isn't quite as sophisticated as yours. Since they're already into this, they are throwing gobs of money at your enemies hoping that they can delay you for a while, at least long enough so that they can get their product out first, that way they can rake in the lion's share of the profits."

The shock showed on Ellie's face as she said, "Christ, what in the hell have we gotten ourselves into here?"

Nash went in the other direction, he said, "That means we better get the big three together as soon as we can arrange it. All this harassment will die away after we unveil our product. By the way, what are we going to call it?"

"We'll work on that later; let's get this meeting over first. Do you have anything else for us today, Regina?" Ellie asked.

"Do you want us to physically come into Franklin Industries and see what we can find?"

"Absolutely, Mike, see to it that Regina and her people have full access to wherever it is that they want to go."

"We will probably do our best work at night; can we have access to your executive's offices overnight?"

"Yes, everyone is usually gone by seven. If you come in at eight you will have ten hours of freedom to do what you do. Mike, see that they even have the passwords for these people's computers, after all they are the company's computers so we have the right to keep a record of them."

When Mike and Henry left, Regina said, "I have to tell you that, based on what we already have, I suspect either Henry Paterson or Charlie Anderson, but give us a few days and we should have this nailed down for you."

"What makes you think it's Henry?" Nash asked. He wanted to ask about Charlie but refrained from doing so now.

"Two reasons. First, it's how he looks when things like this are being discussed and secondly he has access to everything. How long has he worked for Franklin?"

Ellie thought for a few moments then said, "I think he's been here for about ten years."

"Then likely as not he has ties to Bennington. We'll check it out. Don't alert him, we don't want him to purge his computer just yet. What I would like to do right now is talk to your computer people and have them fix it so no-one can erase anything that's on the computers right now."

Ellie picked up her phone and called Patty Vandershot. They talked for a few minutes then Ellie hung up and said, "It's fixed. When this is over I'd like to treat you to something special."

"Just pay your bill on time and we'll be straight," Regina said standing up, she had a lot of work to do.

"Just the same, you've earned a bonus. What in the hell are we going to do about Mercedes though? They swing a lot of weight in the industry."

"Well, since they haven't come out with any preliminaries yet, you have the inside track. Use it to your advantage," Regina said.

When Regina left, Nash followed Ellie to her office. Once they were seated, Ellie hit her intercom and said, "Get Mattie Sanders in here right away."

"I know what you're going to do," Nash said and smiled at her, then he said "and I approve."

Five minutes later Mattie was seated next to Nash in front of Elli's desk. "Mattie, can you get that one-minute commercial on the air tonight? I want it on all three of the big network channels, hell even put it on Fox. I want the world to know that we have this very useful gizmo for cars and maybe they can put the pressure on the automotive industry and make them come to us."

"What about the Super Bowl commercials?" Mattie asked. She'd put a lot of work in on these ads.

"Start your people on them, make new ones if you have too, but I want this out to the public tonight."

"It's going to be spendy. Do you have a cap on monies?"

"Not tonight. This is going to be a one-shot deal. But if this comes off the way I expect it to, plan on being busy tomorrow with calls from every auto manufacture in the world. If this goes over as big as I expect it to we'll be busy, so set up a full disclosure conference for Friday afternoon in our employee dining hall and invite the press in on this, if they're interested."

"The press is going to want this before then."

"Then give it to them, but not the particulars how it works, that's for Friday."

"So, I guess that means I've see the last of my bed for the next five days," Mattie said as she stood up and rushed from the office all smiles. Yet the truth of the matter was that she really was a workaholic; in fact she loved this sort of pressure.

When they were alone in her office, Niles said, "I can't believe Charlie has anything to do with this shit, we've been friends forever. Never once has he ever come across as being anything except a company man."

"A company man with ties to Fray Bennington. I should have left him fired when I first took over as CEO."

"At any rate, we'll have to keep an eye on him until Regina confirms his involvement in this mess."

"I agree, I'll turn this over to Mike right away."

Chapter Thirteen

That night the Franklin ads were on four separate channels, they were on all the Six O'clock News' Broadcast. It was costing the Franklin Group nearly two million dollars, but it was well worth it to get this product into the mainstream first and that way they could work on the public's perception of it themselves. What this would tell them was that if there was a ground swell against it, they could halt production right away and stop hemorrhaging money. As it stood now they were spending about two hundred and seventy thousand a day on this project, new stuff like this cost lots of money.

The next morning Ellie was a little late for work, only she did this on purpose, she wanted to give both the public and the auto industry time to react to their announcement last night. Even though she expected a response of some sort, there was no way she would have thought it would be as big of a thing as what she ran into. She actually had to call security to clear a way so she could get through the throngs of people who'd gathered at the gates to her buildings.

A few of the questions she did hear and understand were all directed toward the audacity of Franklin Industries to think that they could take humans out of the driving experience. Some were simply protesting to have something to protest about, they were the ones who'd protest against everything from hot coffee in paper cups to perpetuating accusations of Santa Claus being a pervert.

Once she was inside the building and on her way up to her office, perhaps for the first time since working there she felt the stares of her fellow employees, they were all looking at her today. She tried to put on a happy face, but inside she was nervous as hell. Thank God, Nash was waiting for her in her office when she got there. She went directly to him and into his arms.

"What is going on out there?" she asked.

"As close as we can figure this is a good thing. According to Mike they began gathering about three hours ago and it's grown into what you see now. For the most part it's about seventy percent positive. I would have never have figured it was going to be this big of a stir, but apparently it is. The switchboard has been busy too, right now there are about two thousand calls an hour coming in and there again they are mostly positive. I told them to answer every call on the outside chance that one of them might be from one of the Big Three. So far, it's only been the Japanese car makers that are located here in the states and of course the English automakers that have called. I have a list of them on your desk, but you can plan on the others to check in before noon. I do believe we have a hit on our hands."

"Then what in the hell is that mess at the gates?"

He picked up a newspaper from her desk; it had been folded to a specific page, page two. Half of a page was devoted to this story, complete with pictures, probably copied from the commercial they'd aired last night. It was the Free Press again, only this time they were playing the devil's advocate and then answering themselves in a more positive way. For some reason the announcement and article had inflamed some of the public and emboldened others.

After he gave her some time to look the article over, he said, "Well lady, you ready to start making a ton of money today? If you are, then we can begin returning some of these calls and get the ball rolling. For now, we've set the price of each complete unit at two thousand, two hundred dollars. It is costing us a little over half that to produce them, thus giving us an almost fifty percent markup. What this also does is give us some wiggle room to negotiate some really great deals for the right customers. Once we go into full production our cost will drop even lower, but only by a few hundred dollars. Franklin has two patents on this, one for the entire units working gear and the other for the computer that is the brainchild of the unit."

"Do you think we should sell the rights to either of these patens to any country?"

"No, I don't, that's because not all countries will have the same safeguards in place that the U.S. does. Furthermore, I don't think we should sell the rights to produce these units to anyone, we should keep them ourselves. The stock market is opening up in twenty minutes, let's see what our stock does and go from there."

At the close of trading yesterday Franklin stock was selling at forty-seven dollars and fifty-one cents a share. It was holding steady and hadn't changed much after Ellie's take-over several months back.

The two of them headed for the coffee pot and by the time trading started there were eight anxious souls in the office waiting, they were all looking at the TV in Ellie's office. Ten minutes after trading started their stock was climbing off the charts. In less than an hour it was trading at over two-hundred and thirty dollars, U.S., a share and there was no telling what it was doing overseas. The three thousand shares that Ellie owned, at the present time anyway, represented nearly seven-hundred thousand dollars. It also meant that suddenly Franklin Industries was a force to be reckoned with. It's worth had quadrupled by noon.

Ellie's first call went to the CEO of Toyota in Torrance, CA. She invited them to be there for the meeting this Friday explaining that all would be reveled and that contracts would be discussed at that time. While she did this, Nash was on the phone with Volvo in Torslanda, Sweden, they were located just outside Gothenburg and he was doing the same thing, inviting them to the meeting Friday.

They were not under any allusions, they knew that the CEO's of these companies would not be there, but hopefully whomever they sent would at least have enough brains that they would disseminate the official word back to them without embellishing on it too much. Suddenly Nash had another of his ideas.

When he hung up, he waited until Ellie was off the phone before saying, "Let's get advertising to put together a pamphlet that we can hand out to our prospective clients. If they show up from an auto company, they get a pamphlet."

In response, Ellie called it in herself. They had two days to get ready for this meeting on Friday; there was no time to waste, not one minute. Her next call went to Patty Vandershot and she tasked her staff with making most of these callbacks. While that was taking place, both Ellie and Nash began drafting up what they were going to say at this meeting. They needed to put their best face forward, they would be speaking to the world and they knew it.

"Let's show that DVD to them, the one Mattie had made up after our trip to Canada, the ten minute one," Nash recommended.

"Great idea, set it up." She then got back to writing out what she intended to say at this meeting. She intended to be the next to the last speaker, Nash would be first, then they'd show the movie and then she'd give her spiel before turning it all over to Mattie.

After that, she'd just have to play it by ear. If things got out of hand, she wanted to be able to have an escape route, that meant security would be needed. That was her next call.

All that day and well into the wee evening hours, or one might say the night, the executives of Franklin were busy. They all had jobs to do, either directly or they had something to contribute to this coming meeting on Friday. Nash stuck his head into Ellie's office at nine that evening and asked, "Can I come in?"

"Yes, and build us a drink, I need one after today."

"Have you eaten anything?"

"I had a sandwich about five, but now that I think about it, I'm starved."

"Are you having fun yet?" he asked, plopping into one of the chairs facing her desk.

She gave him the finger and said, "Go to hell. If I wanted to work this damn hard I'd have stayed a secretary. Today I've been busier than a whore at sea on an aircraft carrier."

"Speaking of a whore, I sure would like to know one right about now. I need to get laid. I'm tighter than spandex pants on Jackie Gleason. Have any ideas?"

"I do, but if I ever catch you with a whore, I'll make an 'it' out of you. Let's go out to eat and then you can take me to your place."

All during the meal they talked about what they'd done today and what all they had to do tomorrow. Friday would be just as hectic, but by that evening they would be set for life or so they hoped. At his place, they made love with reckless abandonment and unbridled passion, they both needed this release. Around midnight she drove home alone and after taking a quick shower she was in bed and sound asleep by twelve-thirty.

Fray Bennington might be out of the picture, but Mercedes wasn't. In the 1980s, Mercedes built the world's first robot car together with a select team at Bundeswehr University in Munich. Partially encouraged by this success, in 1987 the European Union's EUREKA program initiated the Prometheus Project on autonomous vehicles and it was funded to the tune of nearly €800 million. The project was considered a success when, in 1995, a re-engineered S-Class Mercedes took an autonomous trip from Munich in Bavaria to Copenhagen in Denmark and back. On the public highways the robot achieved speeds exceeding 109 mph (this was permissible in some areas of the German Autobahn). The car's abilities heavily influenced robot car research and funding decisions worldwide for Mercedes, but to date no one had developed a car that would drive on any road in existence and none could do all the things that Nash's system would. Nash's brainchild would be the interim between a human driving and a full robotic takeover, but that's not the way Mercedes saw it.

For Franklin Industries to be coming out with this project now, well it would be undercutting them by a good six months. That meant that all the money they had spent in development and testing in the past would be for naught. Even the developers admitted that Franklin's entry into this realm was far superior to anything they'd came up with in years. That meant they needed to either discredit Franklin or find some other way of discouraging them from continuing this project, at least until they could come out with their own project.

All this was relayed to Lionel Hammond, CEO of Mercedes USA Headquarters in Montvale, NJ. He, in turn, handed this problem over to Roger Adams, a despicable corporate headhunter that was located in Detroit. It was through him that Fray had been in contact with Mercedes, not with the company themselves and it would be through him that the final solution would be carried out, whatever it might be.

"Benny, old pal, I have a job for you and it is a rush job so get over here. We need to speak face to face," Roger said into his phone. He was seated in the den of the Grosse Pointe house that he presently lived in. The house was right next to a VP for Chrysler and of course across the street from Lakeshore Drive was Lake St. Clair itself. This was definitely the high rent district of the Detroit area, tho Roger didn't own this house. He leased it from an out of work automotive swill that still owned it, but couldn't afford to live there anymore. The owner was living in his cottage in Charlevoix, another ritzy area, until he could secure another high paying position after being terminated. What this owner didn't know was that he was through in Detroit, the word was out on him that he'd stole most of his ideas from the people that worked for him. Nevertheless, the rent on this house was twenty-five hundred a month and that wasn't hay. But with what Mercedes was paying Roger to spy on other auto manufactures and with what GM paying him to do the same thing, he made a good living and was able to sock most of his income into an offshore account.

In fact, it was through Fray Bennington that he was able to directly contact the canary in Franklin Industries and what he told Roger today unnerved him. "The meeting with the press and other auto people in the industry is taking place tomorrow. This is where they are going to officially present this new groundbreaking system to the world."

After hanging up, it took Roger an hour to come up with a scheme to cast a little discredit to these proceedings. That's what Benny would be doing tomorrow, Benny and ten others, they were professional dissenters.

For what Roger was proposing that Benny do, most likely he would be tossed in jail again, but he was no stranger to that place, he'd been tossed in jail numerous times in the past. Benny and his people would be the sandpaper for any meeting or rally that they attended. No matter what the speaker said, he and his troupe took the completely opposite side or opinion.

Chapter Fourteen

If Thursday could have been called busy, then Friday morning was a madhouse. Franklin Industries was doing its level best to put its best face forward, but it was hard. Since they were not a public geared company, not in the truest sense of the word, they were winging it in their preparations for the public accommodations they'd invited in today. Most of the time they dealt directly with specific automotive companies like Ford, GM, or Chrysler, not the public in general. Consequently, the press didn't know all that much about Franklin Industries and its name was not generally known by the everyday man on the street.

Ellie was everywhere at once barking out orders and so were the rest of the VP's at Franklin. A lot hinged on this new project, it was the one that would propel them to the forefront of a new and highly competitive industry. This was almost as important of an invention to the automobile as the wheel was. Mankind, for the past hundred years anyway, had taken to driving a car as a rite of passage, a necessity, a part of life, but in one fowl swoop there was going to be a new way that things would be done in this world, especially if this type of technology was adopted and embraced.

The fact that this idea had come from Nash wasn't going unnoticed either. If the idea and concept of this system advanced like the executives at Franklin expected, and was accepted by the public and automotive manufactures alike, then he was in line to become a multi-millionaire several times over. Since he'd developed this idea before coming to work for Franklin or more directly, Ellie, he would be receiving a five-dollar commission on every unit sold. If Franklin sold a mere one million units, then he'd, in-turn, receive five million dollars right off the top. Perhaps that was the reason he was in even worse shape than Ellie was today and even he was barking orders to everyone, which for him was out of character. To say he was nervous would be under estimating that statement by at least a factor of a hundred.

At eleven-forty that morning, one-hundred and twenty guests were shown into the staff-dining hall. There weren't that many seats in the hall, but what the hell, they'd just have to make do, it was the largest public room there was at Franklin's, Piedmont Building. At this complex, there were five buildings in all, the Piedmont was their Corporate Headquarters tho it was not the largest structure they had. The other buildings held various production and assembly lines so they were out, even tho they were larger in size. No matter what there were various security concerns with bringing outsiders into any of the buildings, but they'd just have to make the best of what they had.

Since this was his baby, Nash was the first speaker to take the podium and while he spoke, several of the guests kept interrupting him during his speech and were continually tossing negative connotations towards his invention. Finally, Mike's people took charge, they swooped in and physically removed the agitators and this event seemed to delight most of those present. Of course, all this was recorded by the press, they would never miss a chance to put something like that on the air.

Nash tried to stay away from getting too technical in his presentation, after all these were not engineers, they were businessmen and reporters. Then he showed the ten-minute movie Mattie had made. When the movie was over, several of the businessmen and all of the reporters wanted copies of it so they could show it to their bosses or directly to the public.

The next speaker was Ellie and she spoke about the positive aspects of Franklin's commitment to providing a far more superior system than anyone else had out there and best of all the strongest selling point was that every nut and bolt of this unit had been made right here in America. While Nash and Ellie made good their escape, they tossed Mattie into the lions-den, so to speak, it was her job to handle these people and she did too, she was a master at it.

"Were you nervous," Nash asked Ellie as they made off to her office.

"Shit, I'm still shaking. I am not a public speaker. And don't come up what that shit about it getting easier the more I do it, that was the last time I'm ever going to do that. I'm a CEO, not a fucking politician."

Once they were in her office, she asked, "So how do you think it went?"

"After we got those hecklers out of there, it went rather good, I think. They looked interested and judging from the request for copies of that test movie Mattie made, almost everyone likes what they are seeing."

"You don't think there is any way they can take that DVD and show it in a way that would be negative, do you?"

"I don't think so; it really is an upbeat sort of program. What's going to make it hard to splice different scenes together is the music soundtrack that's on the DVD, it blends together with the action."

They were still talking when Mattie came in an hour later. The three of them built themselves a drink and sat in the conversation setting section of Ellie's office.

"The reporters were all nice, well most of them anyway. The business people that where there were more than interested and they all wanted copies of that DVD to show their bosses, so I provided one to each of them. I told the press that they would only get one if you approved it, thank God you had already made good your escape."

The intercom on Ellie's desk came to life, it was Bobby. "Can I come in?" she asked.

In answer Ellie went over to the door and opened it. "What's up?" she asked as Bobby came into the room and closed the door behind her.

"Just as you suspected, they all checked in within the past hour. As it stands now you have three Saturday appointments at their offices. Ford is for ten, Chrysler has the noon spot and GM is on tap for three. I also have request out there from most of the other CEO's of the rest of the automobile manufacturing world as well."

"Let them stew, cancel those appointments and reschedule them because I'm not going to them, they are coming to me. Give Ford the nine o'clock slot, Chrysler ten, and GM the eleven o'clock appointment. Then schedule the rest in for Monday afternoon and Tuesday starting with Toyota and then go by their ranking all the way down to the Russian's Kam AZ, double them up if necessary. The bottom line is this, tomorrow I'm out of here by noon and I won't be back until eight o'clock Monday."

After Bobby left, Mattie asked, "Are we really going to sell these units for under two grand? I think if we doubled that amount they would still sell like hotcakes."

Ellie looked at Nash; he got up and went to use her in-house phone. "Bobby, would you please get hold of Charlie Anderson, and Henry Paterson and ask them to join us in Miss Masterson's Office?"

Five minutes later the five of them were discussing the pros and cons of raising the price on each unit sold. Charlie came up with a good point, "The actuating gear for the larger, heavier vehicles will cost more to produce. I don't think that a one-size-fits-all, single unit price, would be the right way to go. We should charge a different fee for the heavier vehicles than we do for a Fiat."

"I agree," Ellie said. "What do you think about charging two thousand three hundred dollars for the lighter rigs and then we could increase the cost by two hundred dollars for every five hundred pounds in vehicle weight?"

That meant that a Ford Fiesta, a vehicle that only weighed about twenty-eight hundred pounds, or a Mini Cooper at twenty-six, would come in at the bottom end of this scale while Ford's husky F-450 Super Duty pickup truck would top out at around sixty-seven hundred pounds, meaning it would pay an extra eighteen hundred dollars per unit.

That's when Henry said, "That would be robbery and we all know it. We can produce the units that would operate that heavy of a truck for right around two grand and you want to charge the customer four thousand dollars per unit. I think we need to re-think this before we price ourselves right out of the market."

"I agree," Nash said and right behind him Charlie said the same thing.

"Alright, then we set the price for a small car at fifteen hundred, and the top end at twenty-five. We'll make our money through volume, not individual unit cost. Either way we stand to make a goddamn fortune with this," Ellie said. "But make them understand that they are paying the taxes on each unit we sell, we are not taking the hit on that account," she added.

~♥~

When Ellie and Nash left the building at four-thirty, they were ready for a little relaxation. They stopped at the Happy Wok on Stadium Blvd for an early supper, then went to a movie theater and watched "Saving Mr. Banks" staring Emma Thompson and Tom Hanks. It was nearly ten when they let themselves into Nash's apartment, only to be met by five men about the size of elephants.

"What the hell is this?" Nash demanded, when one of the men grabbed Ellie and pushed her onto a nearby chair, then stood over her, preventing her from rising.

"You need to rethink your job choices. You should be working for the sanitization department, not Franklin Industries, they are going to be broke soon," one of the men said, while two of them grabbed Nash's arms.

Nash flew into a frenzy and broke the hold that the man holding his left arm had. With a free hand, he swung a haymaker at the man holding his other arm, but he didn't break the grip the man had on him. Quickly, the other two stepped forward and they secured his hands behind his back by using duct-tape.

That's when all five of them took turns beating the living shit out of him. First one would work over his face and torso with their fist, then another would take over and do almost the same thing and they did this five separate times, they all had a go at him.

While this beating was taking place, the man standing over Ellie changed once or twice, but she never moved and had enough presence of mind to stay still and keep quiet, no sense making it worse than it already was.

After five minutes of this, Nash was nothing more than a blood covered blob that couldn't stand up anymore. Two men picked him up and sat him on one of the kitchen chairs, then they taped his ankles to the chairs legs and re-taped his hands to the back legs of the chair.

Just when Ellie thought that she was going to escape their attention, two of the men picked her up by her arms and carried her over to the table. As yet she hadn't said a word, but now she had no illusions about what was going to happen next, she was never that naive. With one swoop of his enormous arm, a man swept everything from the table onto the floor. They then bent her over the table and using the same tape they used on Nash, they secured her wrist and ankles to the table. While they did this another man searched in the drawers in the kitchen until he found what he was looking for, a pair of scissors. Moments later Ellie was naked, her clothes cut to pieces and laying on the floor next to the table.

While the men kept Nash awake and made sure he was watching, each man in turn raped Ellie, even her anus received their brutal treatment. When one of them finished and had ejaculated, the next one would use one of several one liter of bottles of soda pop that Nash kept on hand for mixed drinks, on or rather in her as a douche. He'd shake it up, shove the opening into her pussy then let the pop fizz up inside her before he'd take his turn at her. For nearly an hour she had to endure their filth and enjoyment, but she kept telling herself that she'd live through it, tho it was a hard sell every time one of them forced himself into her.

All the while they did this; they had Nash by the hair and continued making him watch them as they took their turns at Ellie. He was beyond resisting, he was barely conscious, but he watched and several times had to spit the bile and blood from his mouth that somehow materialized there.

Finally, the last of them was dressed and after knocking Nash unconscious and breaking his jaw in the process, they left. Ellie lay there for a few minutes and then began to struggle to see if she could get free, but it was impossible. Finally, she did the only thing left for her to do; she began screaming as loudly as she could.

She was nearly hoarse before she heard a knock at the door. "Hello, this is the police. Open the door."

"Help, we are tied up," she shouted, though not very loudly.

One of the cops kicked the door open and as soon as they saw Ellie tied to the table and Nash lying on the floor with his face beaten to a pulp, they called for an ambulance and freed Ellie. She immediately went into the bedroom and came out moments later wearing Nash's robe. The police had already told her not to shower; they said that a rape kit would have to be used on her first.

She felt dirty, but she was alive. Now she turned her attention to Nash, he was really in a mess. There was blood everywhere near him and it was all his.

The aid car that responded took her and Nash to the University of Michigan's Medical Center where they put them into separate rooms. Moments later, they took Nash into an operating room and the first thing they did was ascertain how much damage had been done internally. While they did this, another doctor began to repair his broken jaw and nose.

Meanwhile, Ellie was issued the SAFE Rape Kit and then two nurses helped her use it. Finally, after she was finished, she was allowed to take a shower. She spent nearly twenty minutes in the shower and when she came out to the nurse's station she was wearing a hospital gown and robe.

"How is Mr. Gibson doing?" she asked.

"He's still in surgery. As soon as we know something we'll let you know. Why don't you have a seat over there in the waiting room?"

Alone and with time to think, she remembered the assault on her and even though there were no outward signs of her abuse, she still felt them inside her and them expending of their filth into her. To her way of thinking, the assault was the worst thing that had ever happened to her. She'd given her body over to men who did things to her she'd like to forget, but it had been her choice and at any given moment she could have stopped it, but this was different. She had no control of this assault and even though they had hurt her, she'd remained quiet lest she encourage them to be mean and really hurt her bad. All this had crossed her mind as she lay there on that table and endured those men shooting their foulness into her, time, after time, after time.

Then something else occurred to her, apparently they didn't know she was Nash's boss, the CEO of Franklin. What would they have done to her if they'd have known that? They must have figured she was nothing more than Nash's girlfriend, which she was, but that's as far as their thinking went. Her debasement was more for Nash's benefit than their pleasure. Nevertheless, she'd been repeatedly raped and something like that leaves a lasting impression on the hapless victim, Ellie was no exception.

Finally, after two and a half hours of sitting there alone a doctor came out and took Ellie into a small room with him. "Are you his wife?" he asked.

"No, his girlfriend and boss, how's he doing?"

"Are you the one who was raped?"

"I am, but what does that have to do with anything, how's he doing?" She was getting a bit perturbed by his stupid questions.

"He'll live. He has a bruised liver and his stomach was torn from its connection with the spleen. We repaired it then rewired his broken jaw and reset his broken nose. We have him under heavy medication right now and that's to keep him unconscious. We're doing that so his body will begin to repair all the damage that has been done to it. If he moves around, he may re-tear the spleen again. We will keep him sedated for about two days. He also has numerous bruises and contusions, but they are all minor in relationship with the other damage the body sustained in the beating. Why don't you let us take a look at you and make sure nothing is amiss?"

"I'm alright. I was raped; it's that plain and simple. I didn't fight them so I doubt if anything's wrong with me internally. Let's keep our eye on Nash though. When can I see him?"

"He's in recovery now. You can see him if you like, but I must warn you he looks a lot worse than he really is."

"I still want to see him."

She was rather taken aback seeing him. There were tubes and wires running into and out of him, they were all over the place. His skin was so bruised and bandaged in so many places that he was nearly unrecognizable. They had even shaved part of his scalp and had probes connected to the bare spots, probably to monitor his brainwaves. Meanwhile various machines clicked, buzzed and beeped in the room while a nurse was in and out every few moments to check on him. Ellie, once she was alone with him, leaned over his battered body and said, "I still love you mister so you better get well fast."

Chapter Fifteen

The eastern sky was getting light when she let herself into her home, alone and she was feeling alone too. Before she could get to her suite, Gina appeared in her nightclothes. "Are you alright?" she asked looking at how her boss was dressed.

Ellie gave her a half-assed smile and said, "I'll live. Please draw me a bath while I undress." When she was comfortably situated in the tub, she said, "We had a little problem last night, Mr. Gibson was beaten half to death and I was raped. I've just spent the last five hours at the University Hospital. All I want to do now is relax and get a few hours sleep, I have some very important meetings to attend this morning, so make sure I'm up by eight. The clock on Ellie's nightstand informed Gina that it was already six o'clock.

Ellie hadn't gotten very much sleep, but she was at the office for her first meeting with Ford's CEO, Alan Multan. If he noticed that she was tired, he didn't say anything, but she was exhausted before the day even started. After holding the same meeting with Sergio Marconi of Chrysler and GM's Mary Bara, she headed straight for the hospital. In those three hours of meetings she'd made over five hundred million dollars for Franklin. Now then all they had to do is produce these units in the time frame that she'd quoted them.

The hospital staff had moved Nash into Intensive Care by the time she got there and a few of the machines were now gone, that had to be a good sign. She sat with him for a spell holding his hand and during this time she got all the latest updates from his nurses and even spoke with a doctor, no change; he was still being sedated for his own well-being. Satisfied that he was in good hands, Ellie headed for home and went directly to bed; she was wiped out and needed to shut her eyes for a few hours.

As soon as Ellie left Nash's room, Regina came storming into the hospitals offices and demanded to know what was going on with her friend. When she'd first heard about this latest turn of events, she had dropped everything and headed straight for the hospital. After spending an hour there in and around Nash's room and scaring the living daylights out of the staff, she left and headed for Ellie's, but was turned away at the door by a very insistent Gina. She said that her boss wasn't to be disturbed until suppertime and she told Regina that this was directly from Ellie herself.

"Tell her that I'll be back," was all that Gina got and with that said Regina was gone.

Ellie was just getting out of yet another shower when Regina showed up so she waited in the study for her new friend. Ten minutes later a very tired looking Ellie showed up and for the next half hour she related what'd happened to her and Nash less than twenty-four hours ago, she even told Regina about the meetings with the big three automakers.

Gina stuck her head in the room and said, "Dinner is served, Miss Ellie."

"Come on, you're eating with me. Gina, set another place, will you?"

But Regina was one-step ahead of her boss, she'd already told Gina to do so. When the two women sat down at the table, Regina started with the questions, questions that the cops would likely as not ever ask.

Elli's answers went something like this and it was said between mouthfuls of her meal.

"One of them had LOVE and HATE tattooed on the fingers of his huge hands."

"LOVE was on his right hand, HATE on the left."

"Yes. I could smell beer and garlic on one of their breaths. Two of them had long hair that was down to their shoulders, although one's was tied back in like a pony-tail. Three of them had brown hair, one was a redhead and he had his hair cut really short. The man with his fingers tattooed, his dick was sort of small and it didn't hurt me at all, in fact after the others got through with me, I barely felt him at all."

"It was the one with the pony-tail that hit Nash that last time and knocked him and the chair over. It was a vicious blow; I could hear it really clear. While they were raping me, I saw all of their hands and all five of them had bloody knuckles."

"They were all built like linemen for the Detroit Lions."

"No, they didn't talk that much once the rape started. I did hear one say, 'come on, hurry up, we haven't got all night you know', but I don't know who said that."

"No, it was just rape for me. Nash took the brunt of their punishment. But believe me, that rape was enough. I've never felt so violated in my life, or helpless."

"You bet your ass I'd like to have some alone time with them. I'd like to let them know what it feels like to be raped and then I'd like to cut their fucking balls off."

By this time the meal was over and the dishes were cleared. The two women went into Ellie's study for an after-dinner drink and to talk about happier things. Twenty minutes later Regina was gone and Ellie headed for the hospital again.

For something like this Regina's sources were much more extensive and 'in-the-street' than the cops were. She went directly to downtown Detroit and together with two of her operatives, they went to work.

When Ellie walked into the hospital, two doctors were coming from Nash's room. "Well, what's the verdict?" she asked, catching them unawares.

The doctor that she recognized from last night said, "He's doing much better than expected and we are going to bring him out of his sleep tonight. The nurse will be in directly to get the process started."

"How long will this process take?" she asked.

"Between one and two hours, if you like we can call you when he's conscious."

"You won't have to, I'll be right there." And she was too.

At first, he was groggy and couldn't focus his eyes, but they got better and fifteen minutes after waking up he was fully awake. It was during this process that he remembered what they'd done to his Ellie. His jaw hurt like hell, but there was Ellie and she was holding his hand and she was able to kiss his badly bruised face.

One thing was for sure, he woke up with his humor intact, the first thing he said to her, through clinched teeth of course, was, "Hey lady, want to get laid by an ugly troll?" and even that hurt, but he needed to say something to his woman.

"No, but I would like to get laid by my lover. How do you feel?" she asked, with concern written all over her beautiful face.

"I don't rightly know. I am going to have to move a little in order to give you the full 4-1-1 on that account. My jaw feels like hell and I probably look like a train ran over me, did it?"

"Yes and no, and you lay still. The doctor said that if we can't keep you quiet and still, that he's going to put you back to sleep for a week, so be good and don't move around."

"I love you, beautiful lady and I'm sorry for what happened to you. Did they hurt you very bad?"

"Only my pride and my self-esteem, I'll live," but that wasn't the entire truth. She felt those things and much more, things like ashamed, abused, degraded, out of control, embarrassed and a dozen or so other feelings all at once. Though she did notice one important thing, the more time that passed, time that was moving her away from the actual rape, the impact of such a violent act was subsiding to some extent. When it first happened, it was all she could think about, but now, after a mere twenty-four hours, she was able to think of other people and worry about things not related to that horrific event. She'd never forget what those men did to her, but it was not going to ruin her life, she wouldn't let it.

Meanwhile, Nash was working through his own set if demons. He hated those men for what they did to him and if the truth were known, he hated them even more for what they'd done to Ellie. However, there was another set of problems he was dealing with, and that was being forced to watch what they did to the love of his life. They had defiled something that was his and his alone, they had taken something from him. It was something that was very basic and it went right to the very core of his being. Ellie was his woman; she was his exclusively, just as he was hers. Those men had expended their filth into her and on her. He knew she'd wash and clean herself up, but would their relationship ever be the same as it had been two days ago? He had some serious hurtles in his mind to overcome in the next few days. The one thing that had not diminished though was his concern for her wellbeing.

"I love you, lady," he said through clenched teeth.

She kissed him again and said, "I love you too, now be still."

He lay there with his hand in both of hers and so long as they were touching it seemed to be making everything alright. They began to gain strength from one another and as they did, Ellie's face took on a much healthier look, her eyes brightened and the cruel set she had about her mouth lessened, she looked much more normal. They were good medicine for each other, they needed each other and they were in love once more.

Regina's first real break occurred Sunday morning. While most of the godly citizens of this state were in church, Regina was sitting in a crack house with nine other lost souls watching them mellow out. One of the crack-heads told her, "Yeah, I know about this bunch of ex-jocks. They mostly break heads for two shylocks who operate out of the Arcade Bar and Grill on Michigan Ave. I've seen this bunch; they look like the offensive line of the Lions. What do you want with them?"

"Do you think they actually played professional ball?" she asked.

"I doubt it, they're not the type. These guys are mean, but only when they travel in a pack. They may have been strong once, but they're mostly fat now. Hell, I bet I could take on one of them if he was by himself. Don't misunderstand me, together they are nothing to fuck with."

"Thanks." Regina stood up and dropped two twenties onto his lap and then she left. Once she was in the safety of her huge Ford Van, she called in three of her men. They left their vehicles in a park-and-ride by the Greyhound Bus Station in downtown Detroit and got into her rig.

"What's up boss?" Derrick asked.

"I have a good lead on this bunch. Do any of you know anything about the Arcade Bar and Grill on Michigan Ave?"

From the back seat she heard, "Yeah, it's sort of a dump, but at one time it was really a nice place. They dance to the jukebox on the weekends and it wouldn't surprise me if the gals that come in there weren't hookers."

"That's where we're going. We're going to go in one or two at a time, I'm going in alone. How big is the bar?"

"It's a long one. It's on the left and runs the entire length of the joint."

"Do we need brass knuckles to get in the joint?" she asked.

"Maybe, but I doubt it at this time of the day."

"I'm going in first and spend about forty-five minutes there, then two more of you come in and I'll leave. Later on if we haven't got our pigeons by this time, I'll go back in with one of you thugs, hopefully around shift change so they won't recognize me. Do me a favor and sip your drinks, don't gulp them down. Just because we are on an expense account doesn't mean we need to be drunk when and if they do show up. If they do show up, use your cell and buzz the rest of us."

"What are we going to do with them if they do come in? There are five of them and only four of us?" one of her men asked.

"Well it's this way. One of us is going to pick a fight with one of them and then when he or they come outside I'm going to stick a fucking gun in their faces. We put them in the van and take them to that empty warehouse over on Jefferson Ave, the one that Motown Recovery used to use. Surprisingly, I still have a key to the side door. Listen, don't take any chances with these pricks, I don't want any of you hurt. At the first sign of any real danger we back off and think of something else."

Regina got out of the van and went into the tavern alone.

Chapter Sixteen

By Monday Nash was in good enough shape to be released from the hospital and sent home, but only if he stayed in Ellie's care. Once outside the hospital he got out of the wheelchair on his own, walked the two steps to her car and stiffly got in, but it wasn't easy. His midsection still hurt a lot and the stitches pulled, the stitches they put in after his operation. He could now open his lips enough to talk and get a straw into his mouth so that he could drink his meals, but his jaw was still wired shut. It's true that he was able to talk, though it was strained and after only a few minutes he had to rest, the mere vibration of his voice caused the jaw to hurt like hell.

Once in Ellie's house, Gina took over and waited on Nash hand-and-foot. Finally, he had to ask Ellie, "So when were you going to tell me that you made it to the Saturday meetings?"

"When you were stronger and could talk better. Yes, I made the deals and all three of them wanted in. I sold sixteen million to Ford, fifteen point two million to GM and thirteen point six million to Chrysler. Right now, I have about half of the executive staff making deals with the rest of the automotive industry around the world. Now all we have to do is get into production, its cash on delivery. You know how that works. Today most of the executive staff is closing deals with the rest of the industry."

In his mind he ran the numbers. Even without the vehicle weight offset, she'd brokered an outlay of forty-four point eight million units which would be bringing in over thirty-four billion dollars. After cost outlays and stock adjustments, and let's not forget taxes, that many units would probably net them well over sixty billion in gross profits and that's just the big three, no telling where the rest of the world would weigh in at. That also meant that he was a multi-millionaire too, maybe even around a billion to start with, tho he'd have to wait and see what the IRS did to him.

"We are going to need a bigger factory, one that has at least six complete lines and a bigger shipping bay," he said.

"I thought that too. That's why I have Henry over in Detroit looking for just the right place to buy. At first, I was thinking of renting, but if this goes the way I think it's going to, I want to own our own facility and that way we won't be at the mercy of some asshole landowner."

"Have you heard from Mercedes yet?"

"Yes, even they have made a call. I asked Patty Vandershot to handle them personally, but this isn't over yet, not by a long shot," she said, as a cloud fell over her expression and her voice changed.

"I know you. What are you doing?" he asked.

"Right now, I don't know for sure what's going on, but Regina is in Detroit and she's hot on the case."

"Christ, knowing her she's liable to kill those bastards just because. Can you give her a call and ask her to come visit us?"

"I talked with her yesterday and she said something about being hot on their trail, but so far they were a no show, whatever that meant. At any rate she's due to call in around five this evening, you can talk to her then if you're awake and able."

~♥~

Regina was still in downtown Detroit and they were long past trying to be just another customer. Her white van was now parked directly in front of the bar and the boys had retrieved their rides as well. Now they were taking turns sitting in the back of the van where the windows were tinted enough that they couldn't be seen unless someone came right up to the van and looked inside. Two people were on watch from the time the joint opened at ten in the a.m. until two a.m. when the bar closed. For sixteen hours they switched from one team to another in two-hour shifts and this had been going on for two days. It was getting old really fast. While one member of the team stood their watch, the other would make toilet visits, go for coffee or leave to get something to eat, or just get away from the boredom of what they were doing. They'd started this stakeout around noon Sunday and it was already Monday evening, but the five men they were looking for had been a no-show, at least so far.

"Keep a sharp eye, I have to make a personal call to our boss and check in. I'll be back in about fifteen minutes," Regina said, crawling between the second row of seats and opening the sliding door on the right side of the van. She went across the street to Paul's car, got in and made her call using her personal cell phone.

After talking with Ellie for a few minutes, Ellie handed the phone to Nash. "Hey boy, it's good to hear your voice again, but you need to take your head out of the toilet so I can understand you," she teased.

"Where are you at now?" he asked.

"Downtown Detroit?"

"Do you have a company of National Guard Troops with you? That's the only way I'd go down there at this time of day."

"No, though we do have a lead on those men and we're following it up. Listen you dipshit, you stay still and get better.

I'll be by one day this week and we can chat, but for now let me talk to Ellie."

Nash handed the cell phone back to Ellie and he listened to her side of the conversation.

Pause: "Yes, I would like a chance to talk to those good-old-boys before the cops get them."

Pause: "I'll be there within forty-five minutes, day or night."

Pause: "Spend the money. It's worth it to me."

Pause: "Nope, this is coming out of my pocket, not Franklin's."

Pause: "I promise I won't kill them, but they will know who I am by the time I'm finished talking with them."

Pause: "You take care. I don't want any of your people hurt over this."

When she hung up, she looked at Nash, smiled and said, "This isn't over yet, not for me."

Regina was on her way back to the van when she spotted three men that looked out of place in this neighborhood and they were big enough to be called massive. She was sure her man in the van was watching them too, so she approached them and said, "Hey, do you guys know where" ---by this time she was a few feet from them when she pulled her 9mm from her pocket and stuck it in their faces. Her man in the van jumped out and he too was brandishing a weapon.

"Gentlemen, get in the van. We'd like to talk to you," Regina said.

One of the men made a move like he was going to grab at Regina, so she shot him in the fleshy part of his leg. "Now you idiots can make this easy or hard, it really doesn't matter to me one way or the other."

They got into the van without a fuss after that.

Once inside, while Regina held her weapon on them, Paul used duct tape to secure their hands together behind their backs and he also taped their ankles together. With Regina in the third seat still holding a gun on them, Paul got behind the wheel and drove them over to the warehouse. On the way, Regina called her other two men, they were in bed sleeping. "Get over to the bar and take up the watch. We have the first three, but I want those other two."

When she completed that call, she phoned Ellie. "We have three of them and are headed for the warehouse."

Ellie looked at the clock on the wall; it was nearly eight in the evening and getting dark quickly. "I'm on my way and thank you, Regina."

Snapping her phone shut, Regina sat there looking at one of the men's hands, he had his fingers tattooed with love and hate. They had the right bunch, now she was sure of that.

The three men's names that she had were Bill, Joe and Roger; Joe was the one with the tattooed fingers. Almost identical in looks, all three of them were hard pressed as to the why this was happening to them and was even more confused as to who was doing this. They'd had repercussions from some of their boss's clients before, but usually it was in the form of cops arresting them, they'd never been physically attacked before. This was something new to them. None of them weighed quite three hundred pounds, yet, but Jeff, one of the other two not with them tonight, did come close to that.

"Are you going to tell us what the fuck is going on?" Roger asked, he was in the front seat.

"No, I don't believe we are. It's suffice to say that for perhaps the first time in your stupid lives you are going to pay for something you've done. Now shut up or I'm going to stuff the dirty, menstrual Kotex that's in my cunt into each of your mouths and tape it there."

The man that she had shot earlier, this had to be Bill, sat in the seat quiet like and watched the blood ooze from his leg, soaking his pants in the process. It burned like hell, but he wasn't about to give them the satisfaction of knowing it bothered him.

At the warehouse, Paul drove the van inside after Regina opened the door for him. While she did this, two of the three captives tried to escape, but to no avail, they were caught and that was that. Once inside, Paul pulled over to where the office used to be. While he held the gun on their captives, Regina went into the office to see if this was where they wanted to hold her prisoners, it was. There was a larger outer office and a smaller one off to one side. The only chair she found was a really old, broken down office chair that was missing one of its castors. It didn't matter, her guest didn't need to be comfortable, the floor would do nicely. In the small office was a rusting metal shellwalker desk with three of the four drawers missing. Even with the missing drawers the desk was heavy.

Satisfied, Regina pulled the three-wheeled chair out of the office with her and together with Paul, got the first of the three men onto it. With her watching the other two men this time, Paul pushed the first of the men into the outer office and once inside dumped him onto the floor next to an overturned file cabinet without any drawers. Doing some quick thinking, he pulled the man over to the file cabinet and taped his hands to one of the drawer dividers on the front of the cabinet. If this guy was going anywhere, it would be with this file cabinet hanging from his secured hands.

The place sort-of stunk; it was a mixture of mold, whatever had been in here years ago and of course tons of dust. It was filthy at best and there were spots out in the main part of the warehouse that had stagnate, smelly, standing water on the concrete floor. Once all three of her captives were lying on the filthy floor, Regina rechecked their bindings, then she called the bar to see what her other men were doing.

"How's it going?" she asked.

"Vic checked, they are in there and are sitting with two other men at a table that's next to the back wall. If we go in hard, it's going to be difficult to dig them out of that corner without someone getting hurt."

"I think I would like to have those other two men as well. Send Tom over so he can watch this bunch with Paul, then I'll come over and see if I can get them to come outside with me. You never know, they may just be that shallow and stupid."

Twenty minutes later Regina got out of Vic's car, unbuttoned two of the top buttons of her blouse and went inside. She went directly over to the table where the four men sat and said, "Hey, my brother owes you guys two yards, but he doesn't have the cash right now. He was wondering if you'd take his car in exchange for the money he owes you."

All four of them looked at Regina like she was something to be discarded after diner. One of the bosses, the slender black skinned man asked, "What sort of car are we looking at?"

"A '04 Ford Crown Vic that's in perfect shape, no rust or anything."

"I guess we could have a look," the white man said and the four of them stood up. They followed Regina out the door. Once outside, there stood two other men and suddenly Regina was holding a gun on them. Another of Regina's men pulled a weapon from behind his back, it'd been tucked in his belt and this time they were looking at the dirty end of a beautiful 1911 Colt .45 so they stopped and listened.

The men were quickly moved off to the side of the building before Regina said, "We'll put all four of them in the van, you guys can come over later and pick up your cars. Larry, go inside and make sure everything looks natural, we don't want to make too many waves."

Like the other three, these men were not used to being accosted like this, that's because they were usually the ones striking fear into people. They were not scared easily, but these people with the guns were getting on their nerves nevertheless.

Once they were in the van, it was the other boss, the white man, who did all the talking.

"What's up with all the cloak and dagger shit?" he asked.

"You'll see," Regina said, from her seat in the back of the van.

"Do you people have any idea who the fuck you're dealing with?"

"We know exactly who we're dealing with and unless you shut that fucking hole in your face and keep quiet, I'm going to stuff his shit stained underwear in it. Do I make myself understood?" She was indicating one of the other men trussed up there.

The rest of the trip was quiet.

When they got to the warehouse they spotted Ellie, she was walking around looking for a way into the building. Regina pointed to the overhead door. When Ellie got to the van, Regina said, "Bring your wheels inside, if you leave them out here it'll be stripped before you get the door closed behind you. Follow us."

Ellie was wearing an old pair of jeans, walking shoes, a dark blue poplin shirt and had her hair covered with a baseball cap. Even with this garb on, she looked like she'd just stepped from the pages of Vogue.

Once they had all the men in the office with the others, Regina, and her four cohorts stood over them and waited for Ellie, this was her show from here on out. Like Regina, Ellie went into the small office, looked around and spotted the rusting desk. Satisfied with what she saw, she went back into the outer office and stood before the seven huge men before saying, "Do you gentlemen remember me?"

Suddenly a look of comprehension came across two of the men's faces, but they kept still, no sense making things any worse. Ellie saw the looks and that's why she chose one of those two men first. "Could you guys take this one into that office and tie him onto that desk in there, face up. I need to get a few things from my car before I join you back there."

A few moments later she walked through the outer office carrying two plastic shopping bags and a baseball bat. That prompted the black man to say, "Now what in the hell is going on here?" In answer, Ellie hit him in the head with the bat, knocking him out. That ended any further protest from the others.

In the small office, Ellie said, "Leave him here with me, I'll be alright." Paul left and joined the others in the outer office. She would be alright, but she couldn't attest to her captive's wellbeing. After rechecking his bindings, she said, "You do remember me, don't you?"

"Yeah, you're that broad we banged this past weekend, Friday I think it was."

"Right, give the man a golden star. But now it's my turn to have some fun. You up for this?"

"For what? If you're smart you'll turn us loose and forget this ever happened."

"But I can't forget. You didn't give me any choices, did you?"

"What we did was for your boyfriend's benefit, it wasn't all directed towards you."

"Oh, but it was. You see, I was the object of your enjoyment. Needless to say, I did not enjoy it, not one bit. But I am going to enjoy this."

From one of the plastic bags she pulled out a handball and even though he protested, she eventually got the ball into his mouth and then she taped his mouth shut with the ball in there. With him silenced, she next pulled a pair of scissors from the bag and cut his pants and underwear from his body. With him exposed like this, she slipped her hands into a pair of latex gloves and picked up his flaccid manhood. "My, my, this doesn't seem to look like it did last Friday. But we'll see what we can do to rectify that."

Using both hands, she played with his cock a little, she did this until he had a partial hardon. Then she picked the bat up and retrieved a jar of Vaseline from the plastic bag. She used the Vaseline to coat the handle of the bat and while she did this he watched, only in horror this time. Suddenly he knew what was coming next.

Wearing a huge smile, Elli began trying to get the bat handle into his anus. It took several tries but eventually it slipped in past his sphincter and she cruelly shoved about eight inches of it inside him. He was screaming continuously now, but the only one who heard him fully was himself. Oh sure, he squirmed and wiggled, but he couldn't break the bonds that kept him tied to the desk. When the bat entered him, he involuntarily got a full erection and this caused her to smile even larger.

Once more she removed something from the plastic bag, this time it looked like a recital thermometer. Grasping his erection, she jammed the thermometer into the opening at the end of his penis. Once the entire thing was inside him, she said, "I do hope you are enjoying this as much as I did last Friday," whereas she pulled the bat out, turned it around and struck the side of his dick. She didn't hit him that hard, but it was enough to break the thermometer in several places. Even with the handball in his mouth, his screams could be heard, though they were muffled. His face contorted with pain and his body fought to get away from its attacker, but it was for naught.

"This is fun, isn't it?" she asked, but he was beyond listening to anything she was saying. The pain had to be horrendous. But she was done with him so she said "This is what it felt like when you raped me. This isn't directed towards you, it's directed towards your bosses. You can tell them how much fun you had back here some other time; that's because right now I have four more little boys that need to have a lesson taught to them."

Just so he'd remember her the rest of his life, she took the bat and struck him in the balls with it. The pain caused him to pass out.

Stepping over to the door, she opened it and called two of Regina's men in to help her get this lump of meat out of there and bring in the next one. The man she'd just worked over was taken out to the warehouse proper and tied to one of the roof supports. He awoke while they were doing this, but he was beyond fighting them anymore. Lying there, he was crying huge crocodile tears while his groin shot sharp shooting pains into his brain every time he moved.

It took her nearly two hours, but eventually she finished with the last of them. Now it was the two bosses turn, they had to be taught a lesson as well, but she wanted some information from them as well. For the time being, she was out of thermometers, but she made do with a wooden pencil.

The white man didn't tell her anything, but the black man did. He gave up the name of Roger Adams. Regina was in the room for this interrogation, she said, "I've heard about his Adams guy. He's not very nice."

"Do you know how to get hold of him?" Ellie asked the man.

The man taped to the desk gave up the phone number, well at least he told them where it was at on his cell phone and then told them where he lived. He didn't want any more of what Ellie was dishing out tonight. His head still hurt from where she'd hit him a few hours ago.

When they were alone in the room, Regina asked Ellie, "What do we do with them now?"

"The police took statements from me after the rape; they also have a rape kit that they used on me. Take the bastards over to the Gethsemane Cemetery, its right there next to the Detroit City Airport. Tie them to a gravestone and then call the cops and let them have them. I'm done with 'em," Ellie said as she put the rest of the stuff in the trunk of her car and closed the lid.

Chapter Seventeen

Nash was sound asleep when Elli let herself into her suite; tho it was no surprise to her that he was sleeping in her bed, in fact she was happy he was there. She went into the bathroom, undressed and stepped into the shower, she felt dirty again, especially after dealing with those scum-suckers. Even though she was tired, she felt too pumped up to go to sleep right then, so after her shower she went down to her den and built herself a drink. Seated behind her desk, she set her personal problems aside and once more put her business mind to work.

She wasn't sure just how involved this Roger Adams was with what had happened to her last Friday, but she now knew he had direct ties with Mercedes so she had to be a little more careful how she handled this from here on out. She didn't want to rock the boat so to speak, but something had to be done so that this stupid harassment stopped. But wait, she already had an ace in the hole; she had these new units, units that the entire world wanted, including Mercedes. Perhaps Mercedes needed to pay a little more than the rest of the world and if they didn't like that they wouldn't get any at all.

It was late when she went up to bed, Nash was still sawing logs and to her way of thinking this was a good thing. Every single day he looked better than the one before, she hoped that it meant he was healing. After only three days the swelling was nearly gone and the bruises were dissipating as well. She kissed him on his cheek and snuggled up against him. Moments later she was as sound asleep as he was.

~♥~

The next morning Nash came down to the kitchen with her and sat with her while she ate breakfast, and downed her second cup of coffee. "Did you get that personal business taken care of last night?" he asked. His voice was still strained, it was hard talking without moving the jaw, but he managed.

"Yes, I did. I was able to clear up a problem that I was having after our un-wanted, or un-needed work-over last Friday night."

"So, what did my little lady do to fix it?"

"I had Regina find those five men, then I went into Detroit last night and it was my turn to work them over for a while."

"And how did you do that, me lady?"

"It's suffice to say they won't be doing that to anyone else, not for a long time. As an added benefit, I found out who hired them and wouldn't you know it, he has ties to Mercedes. I'm going after him next and then Mercedes, in that order too. I want them to know I'm coming."

"My, my, but aren't we the vicious little minks this morning? Would you do me a favor and sort of play this slow, just until I can join you and have some fun too?"

"No, I'm not waiting and giving them a chance to get at us again. I've already got Regina on this Roger Adams fellow, she said she's heard about him before but she can't remember what it was about. Anyway, I also have Mike working on this, he has a few friends with the Ann Arbor PD and he thought that they might just be friendly enough to share with him any information they have on this man."

"Well, what are you going to do when you do find him, invite him over for tea?"

"No, I'm going to remove his balls and then turn him over to Regina so she can have a go at him. Then, if his body turns up, she'll have to deal with it, but I doubt if it will."

With their injuries such as they were, Ellie and Nash stayed home and watched the final football game of the season on the TV. After their ads aired on the Super Bowl, they really got busy.

For Ellie, the next several days anyway, it seems that she was needed everywhere at once. There was some excitement in the company when new production line finally came on line on Friday, but it took a few days to work out the bugs and then suddenly all of their seemingly unorganized efforts came together. Having Nash on hand would have made things easier for her, but he was still having trouble talking and wasn't able to walk very far without a crutch, or having to sit down and rest.

But then Nash was never one to just sit back and let the world pass him by either. What he did do is put in a call to his football buddies and short of physically doing things themselves, they guarded Ellie from the time she left the house until she got to the office. There were two vehicles with two men in each of them and they followed her limo everywhere it went. And no, he didn't tell her about them, this was between him and his buddies. If they could employ men that looked like football players, then the very least he could do was actually have ex-football players on his side.

Also, like Nash and Ellie, Roger wasn't standing around idle either, he sent people to see if he could get to Nash and eliminate him altogether, but that was nearly impossible. That's because Mike Masters had Ellie's residence surrounded with uniformed guards twenty-four seven. Roger knew he could, one on one, out-whit or over power those rent-a-cops, but what good would that do, then the rest of them would be alerted and he'd have the police to contend with to boot. No, he had to come up with some other way of getting to them. And yes, his people did see the two shadows that followed Ellie's limo everywhere it went and unlike the security guards, these men would not be that easy to muscle.

In the security of his home, a fourth story loft that he'd converted into a sanctuary that he felt safe in, he sought the services of a real honest to goodness sniper, one that could hit a moving target at a mile away. He eventually found one; he was a Frenchman that lived in Quebec. It wasn't until he offered to pay him half a million dollars that the shooter, Paul Fisk, agreed to take the job. What did Roger care, Mercedes was picking up the tab on this anyway so money was no object, at least not now anyway.

~♥~

By going to the streets again Regina was able to come up with a location for her current mark. At any rate she knew a lot more than she did a week ago and surprise, she had a photo of Roger, it was from a surveillance video taken at a Shell Service Station less than two blocks from the address she got from a homeless woman three days ago. All it cost her was a bottle of whiskey and a six pack of beer.

She sat up an around the clock surveillance of the building, installed a couple of cameras at the entrances and hunkered down for the wait. Eventually he'd show up, they always did. At dusk the third day of their stakeout he did just that, he came home from wherever he'd been. He was driving a Mercedes, of course, one that was given to him by his employers probably. Now then, all they had to do is break in and they had him, but this was easier said than done. Yes, Regina and her people had spotted all his protection, the cameras, the motion sensors, the alarms and gas dispensers disguised as sprinklers in the ceilings. If they tried to break in, a debilitating gas would pour out of those dispensers, all the doors would automatically lock, they would be seen and detected by the sensors and cameras and most likely the police would not be far behind, so that fact limited them to a time constraint. Anyway, storming the place was out, it was time for plan B to be put into action.

Holly Martin had worked for Regina about a year ago, but she had only been involved with the company for about two months before accepting a position with a law firm in Troy, a suburb of Detroit. But Regina had the knowledge of knowing Holly wasn't all that happy working with a bunch of ungrateful, demanding, lawyers and being hit on constantly by the partners.

The reason they wouldn't leave her alone was because she was gorgeous. Holly was a natural blond, built like the preverbal brick shithouse and she dressed to the nines all the time. She'd accepted specialty jobs from Regina twice before, jobs that required her to act as the dumb blond bit and gain entry to certain establishments, or to entice a suspect out into the open and she was very good at doing that.

"Hi Holly, it's Regina. Want to earn a few extra bucks?"

"No, I want to come back to work for you. Can you arrange that for me?" Holly asked and was serious. She'd had enough of those assholes she worked with and for.

"I can. What position are you looking for?"

"A full-on investigator. I think I'm ready for this, but that'll be up to you. When do you need me?" She didn't have any allusions, she knew Regina would use Holly's looks and body to her best advantage, but at least this way she'd be getting paid for it and not be expected to give it away to those pricks at the firm.

"Can you be ready to go in a half an hour. I'll have Joe pick you up in the van. I've got a job that's right up your alley, it's perfect for you."

"So, I guess I won't be taking dictation or working with a computer, right?"

"That's right, so dress accordingly, sexy."

"What sort of money are we talking about here?"

"How does six grand a month sound to you? But expect to work some long hours when need be for that kind of paycheck."

"That can be arranged. See you shortly, boss."

Less than an hour later the two women sat in the back of the white van discussing how they were going to get Holly inside that fortress. "Your still on the pill, aren't you?" Regina asked.

"Absolutely. I don't need any complications in my life. But no pills, I use the DMPA shot these days. Should I look forward to getting laid on this job?"

"It might come to that. Will that be a problem?"

"Nope, I just like to know what to expect going into this. I think that if I do have to spread my legs, it should be worth something. Maybe a bonus or extra pay."

"Deal, if it comes to that, it's an extra five spot for every occurrence. But don't take advantage if it or I'll sew that thing shut for you," but she said it with a smile.

Holly smiled back at her boss and got out of the van ready to start work. She got into a car with Jeff and he took her around Rogers fortress, then they went to a restaurant to await a call from Regina's people.

They waited for two days before he came out and went to a popular night club, this was right up Holly's alley.

Wearing a mini skirt that was so short that if she'd have sneezed, her ass would be exposed, Holly walked into the club and headed straight for the bar. In that short span of time she was approached three times before she could get there and she turned them all down. Just like that, she was labeled as a lesbian and most men steered clear of her. And yes, she did see Roger and was glad that at least he didn't look all that bad, in fact he was sort of handsome in an average sort of way. All it took was for her to turn the stool she was perched upon around so he could get a glimpse of her wares and flash him a sweet smile for him to approach her. Two drinks later he invited her to join him at a table, which she did. They danced a few times, but he was no dancer so she ruled that out for the rest of this job. Around midnight and with Holly acting drunk, he invited her to come to see his etchings and of course she accepted.

Regina was in the van watching as Roger drove his car with Holly in the passenger seat, into his underground parking spot. The smile she had on her face reflected her good mood, they had an in.

Inside, Holly was already down to just panties, but she kept saying she was hungry so Roger went into the kitchen to fix her a sandwich or something, tho he had to be careful he didn't burn or break that erection he was sporting. While he was in there, Holly turned all of his security off, then pushed the button on her cell phone signaling Regina's group that it was a done deal.

Less than a minute later Roger was shocked to see Regina and four more of her bunch come swarming into his loft. This sure as hell caused him to lose the hard-on he'd been wearing with pride. At any rate he'd been caught with his pants down and he knew it. With his dick hanging out of his underwear, he was bound and gagged before being taken out to the white van. Once there he had no illusions about what was coming next and he was sure he wouldn't enjoy it either.

Ellie was snuggling with Nash in her bed and was sound asleep when the phone rang. She grabbed the cell off her night stand so it wouldn't wake Nash, but he woke up anyway. "Hi Regina. I take it you have something for me?" she said, smiling at Nash. He quickly stuck his head over next to hers so he could hear the answer.

"I do. Would you believe we have a guest, it's none other than Roger Adams himself? Would you like to be on hand when we play the question and answer game?"

Nash spoke up before Ellie could respond and in a muffled sounding voice he said, "You're damn right we want to be there. Where are you now?"

"We're in a garage on the corner of Forest Avenue and Elm Street. You'll see the white van, its parked on the street. We're in the garage behind the house."

Ellie asked, "Is this a place that the neighbors won't complain about the noise?"

"It is. We'll wait for you then. See you soon."

Nash was moving sort of slow, but he was moving and this was a good thing. He needed to confront someone, anyone, to alleviate the frustration he felt over what had happened to him a little over two weeks ago. He'd been setting around in Ellie's house and stewing in his own juices, with hatred being one of the juices. Revenge was another of those juices, so getting to confront the man who set this up in the first place went a long way to alleviate his discomfort. His face still carried a few bruises and his jaw was still wired shut, his other injuries weren't so visible, but they were on the mend also.

Ellie parked her car behind the van, blocking the driveway, but what did it matter, no one was leaving unless she said so anyway. Regina stepped from the garage door, it was the type that swung open like French doors, not the overhead type and when she saw Nash, she rushed forward to give him a hug. "Well if it isn't Batman, glad you could make it." She turned to Ellie and gave her a smile and got one in return. The three of them entered the garage together and the first thing Ellie noticed was that there were two other men there along with a strikingly handsome looking woman who stood off to the side.

There was something familiar about this other woman, but Ellie couldn't put her finger on it, so she stored that thought away for now and concentrated on the object of this little meeting, Roger Adams. He was duct taped to a rusty looking wrought iron lawn chair with a dirty looking pillowcase over his head. From what the new comers could see of him, he was a smaller man, but very powerfully built, muscular in fact.

"My newest hire," Regina said, as she looked at Holly before continuing to speak, "she's the one who turned our bird out." Then directing her attention back to Roger, she said, probably for his information, "We held off asking him any questions so that you could be in on the answers. I have a feeling that he's going to be cooperative and not force us to use some drastic measures to pull the truth from him. Are you ready to begin?"

From under the hood, Roger said, "You assholes ain't getting shit from me. So, have your fun, but in the end, I will have the last laugh when I catch each and every one of you dipshits and cut your fucking hearts out with a dull meat cleaver. I already know that Nash Gibson's there with Ellie Masterson and that cunt that lured me out of the club. That other voice has to be Regina Williams, is that you Regina?"

"Of course it is and over the course of the next few hours you will tell us what we want to know if you want to live. That's the criteria for this exercise, you give us what we want and you live, but if you lie and make us work for the answers we require, then you're going to die and be stuffed into a furnace somewhere so that stinking carcass of yours can warm some old ladies cat for a few hours." And with that said, she reached over and pulled the hood from him.

He sat there blinking his eyes at the sudden light, then looked around the room. Regina said, "Take a good look because it could be your last if you don't play this game using our rules."

"God, you're such a stupid nigger cunt. If you think for one minute that I don't already know I'll never leave this garage alive, then you're even dumber that I gave you credit for. So, if I don't talk or do, the results are going to be the same. Why don't you just get it over with now and save yourself the effort and spare me the torture of having to listen to your goddamn questions."

Nash spoke up for the first time and said, "But that's where the fun of this game lies. We get to hurt you like you did us and you're right, in the end you die though not before we have extracted our pound of flesh. Well in your case it's going to be a couple of pounds, but you get the drift, don't you."? He turned to Ellie and asked, "So do you want to say or do anything first. Then when you get through, it's my turn." He looked at Roger and said, "Gee, this is a fun game. We should play it more often. You're it this time though."

Ellie stepped forward and took the knife offered her by one of the men standing off to the side. She pulled the crotch of his pants away from his body and cut it from his belt down to his knees on both sides and she did this while he sat there and watched. Suddenly he realized that this was not a fact-finding mission, it was one of revenge. He said, "Wait, maybe we can broker a deal. I have information hidden away that will prove who instigated this witch-hunt. But here's the crutch, only I know where it's at. I'll take you there, but when I turn it over to you, you have to promise

to let me live. Is it a deal?"

She finished cutting his pants and underwear from him and exposing his genitals before speaking. By this time Rogers tuff exterior was showing signs of cracking and coming apart. Regina handed Ellie a pair of black rubber gloves and a black rubber apron that went from her neck down to the floor. She stood in front of Roger while she put them on and while she did this, he never took his eyes off of her for more than a second or two. Next, she reached into her handbag and pulled out a pair of pliers and said, "So which testicle should we remove first, the right or left one?"

"NEITHER!" Roger screamed. "Believe me this stuff that I have on the people who hired me is dynamite. Don't cut me, PLEASE!" So, he was down to pleading after all, all traces of the hardcore killer were out the window for sure.

Ellie turned to look at Nash, he was standing there next to Regina watching. He said, "Take the right one and then we'll see how both you and I feel then."

"For the love of Christ, don't. I'm cooperating fully and am willing to forget all this and that's the truth. Please don't cut me. PLEASE!" he screamed.

Looking around her, Ellie spotted the dirty pillowcase and picked it up. "Open his mouth for me, will you?" she asked two of the men standing behind Roger. They took hold of his jaw and forced his mouth open, whereas Ellie stuffed as much of the case into his mouth as she could. The look of terror was written in his eyes, he knew now that this was going to happen and that was that.

It was Nash that spoke up and said, "What do you say we look at what he has and if it's garbage, we can pick this up where we left off. But the bottom line is he stays here, right where he's at, until we look at the material."

Roger's eyes got big and he shook his head in the affirmative. At this stage, he was willing to do anything to prevent the inevitable. He already knew that someone had worked over the five men he sent to do the deed in the first place so he had no illusions about their convictions or resolve. As he shook his head, he began to relieve his bladder so Ellie stepped away lest he squirt her with urine. Well at least they'd scared the piss out of him anyway. Ellie took the knife and stuck it through one of the holes in the seat of the chair they had him trussed up on. It came up between his legs and then she pulled the pillowcase from his mouth.

"In my home there is a lockbox under the floor, it's under the kitchen sink. After you take everything out of the cupboard, lift the top board out and under it there are two loose boards. You have to pry them out with a knife, but they'll come. The combination to this box is 9-13-4, then around once and stop at 2. Inside there's a key that goes to a locker at the Willow Run Airport, number 308. The stuff is in a red shoebox, there's three boxes in there, please don't take the others, they are insurance for some other projects I have completed."

Regina pulled a piece of paper from her ever present leather brief case and with his hands still tied to the arms of the chair, she had Roger sign the consent form. Then she turned to Holly, handed her the paper and said, "Holly, take Joe with you and the two of you get this taken care of. You should be back here in a couple of hours. Oh yes, bring everything that's in the lock box and the locker at the airport so we can see everything he has," then she looked down at his deflated manhood and smiled.

Once they were out the door, Regina, Nash, Ellie and one of the guards went into the house and built themselves a drink and left Roger to stew in his own juices. They knew he'd try to escape, but Regina was a pro, he was tied up until someone released him and not before.

Ellie turned to Regina, with drink in hand and asked, "So who's house is this anyway, and who's booze are we drinking?"

"It's mine. I don't live here, but the deed is in my name. I let my people use it when need be and over the years we've made that garage virtually sound proof. I like using the garage verses the basement, it's easier to clean up afterwards, we just take a hose to it and that's that. Right now, Joe is living here, but the booze is mine and besides he's a tea totter, he's been sober for three years now.

A little over two hours later Holly and Joe returned and they dumped the stuff they'd picked up on the dining room table. The three of them began going through the stuff, there was close to three hundred thousand dollars in cash along with the other stuff. Nash took the money and stacked it in front of Regina, then said, "The spoils of war."

Inside the red shoebox there were five micro cassettes, the type a phone recorder would use. There was also a player there too so they hooked it up and listened to the first of the tapes.

"Hello Mr. Adams. My name is Mr. Jones and I work for Mercedes Benz of America and I represent the company's president and CEO in Germany. Could we have a face to face in a half an hour at the Starbucks on Michigan Ave in Canton. I'm here at the airport and will be there shortly myself."

"And what is the purpose of this meeting?" Roger asked.

"We have need of someone with your particular skills working for us and are willing to pay handsomely for your participation."

"I'll be there."

There was a quick pause and the sound of a phone being hung up. The next sound was a bit muffled, like it was being filtered by clothing or something like that. They listened to this tape and the next two before Ellie looked at Nash and said, "This stuff is enough to put people in jail and get the Mercedes brand band from doing business in the US."

"Did Mercedes come on board and buy our units?" Nash asked.

"They sure as hell did and to the tune of a hundred thousand units per year. We have a signed contract and everything."

"But I'll bet its contingent with us being able to deliver the units in a timely manner and they are to the advertised standards, right."

"And you'd win, but that's the way almost all of them read. We already have the first three thousand units in boxes and they're in route to the first customer, that's Toyota, then comes Ford. Mercedes is way down on the list, they were one of the last to come onboard."

Regina took this moment to butt-in with, "You do know that all this should be turned over to the FBI and so long as it never leaves my sight, it will be classified as evidence in any court of law. Why not let them go after a company as large as Mercedes. If you go at it alone there's too many pitfalls and the cost would be immense to say the lease."

"Could we get a copy of all this? It should fit on one regular sized cassette tape," Nash asked.

"I think I can arrange that. Then I'm going to take Roger and these tapes to the FBI's headquarters in Detroit and then we're done with it. When Roger and or Mercedes goes to trial, it'll be me on the witness stand, not you two or Franklin Industries, just me. I am a licensed private investigator and that should do the trick."

An hour later when Ellie opened the door to her home, both she and Nash were exhausted, it'd been a long night and early morning, but Roger Adams was now in the hands of the authorities and this nightmare was officially over, or so they thought.

Chapter Eighteen

About the time that the second production line came on line at Franklin Industries, Roger Adams was being charged with no less than seven murders and three times that many counts of other unlawful actions, including strong-arming, theft, and kidnapping just to name a few. When the federal agents tore his apartment apart and using the computer they found there, they came up with the names of other cohorts he was in bed with and then they went after them as well.

Meanwhile, the automotive world was clamoring for Nash's invention. For a few days GM made noises like they were going to sue him because they thought that his invention should legally be theirs, but when he was able to produce that memo and with a formal rejection notice in hand, they knew they didn't have a leg to stand on.

The first of the cars with Franklin and Nash's units in them rolled off the assembly line at the Toyota plant and were being snapped up as fast as they hit the dealers. When some of the manufactures of vehicles came looking for more of these units, they found that the price had grown, nearly double in fact and they were sorry they hadn't ordered them when they were first offered.

For two months, the FBI worked at putting together a case against Mercedes, but so far their transgressions weren't public knowledge and the huge car company was fighting them all the way. However, that all ended when Nash, fully recovered by now, called in the press, one at a time and played portions of the tapes for them. From this point on it became front line news and was the lead story on all the six o'clock news broadcast and the newspapers headlines across the nation began to crucify Mercedes as well.

When the first story hit, the FBI pulled Regina into their offices and asked her where this news leak came from and she honestly told them that she didn't know. "Maybe it came directly from Adams himself," she said.

"We doubt that, Roger Adams was stabbed to death a week ago in the jail we were holding him in. So now what do you say?"

"I have nothing. I swear to you that the leak didn't come from my people, though you might look within. Maybe it was leaked from your office, it's happened before."

And so it went.

Sales of Mercedes fell off to such a point that dealers were looking for new manufactures to supply them with vehicles that didn't have the Mercedes name on them. These days it was more prestigious to own a Cadillac with one of the new units installed in them than a Mercedes. As of yet, Franklin had not delivered a single unit to that German company, they were really low on their list of customers.

With Ellie, Nash and Franklin Industries flying high and with the automotive manufactures throwing money at them right and left, it was bound to happen. The first car with one of these units installed in it was involved in an automotive accident. Tho it was difficult to prove that the accident was the direct fault of the unit. But then, wasn't the human element in the driving experience supposed to have been removed? At least that's what the press was putting out to the public. While the state police continued their investigations, cars continued to pour off the assembly lines and every one of them had a Franklin Industries unit in them. Two weeks after opening a third assembly line at Franklin, a fourth was nearing completion.

While all this was taking place, Nash came up with the idea of installing an automotive sized black box in the vehicles, it was about the size of a pack of cigarettes. This box would be hooked up to the cars computer and a record of the past weeks readings would be available. Then if the information wasn't needed, it would be recorded over, thus eliminating the need to replace these disk with new ones. From start to finish, it took the company three hours to produce a main unit of the vehicles controller, but it only took a half an hour for the black boxes. This two-ounce assembly that was being produced at Franklin was not free, it ended up costing the automotive world four hundred bucks apiece and of course a portion of that money found its way into Nash's bank account too.

And with thousands of these units rolling off the line every day and night, the capitalist in the stock market trade clamored for a piece of the pie, but there was no stock to be had at any price. The private common stock that Ellie and Nash held quadrupled in value and again made them both millionaires, several times over. Since the majority of the stock was held by the Franklin Trust, the board of directors were more than happy with their influx of funds and Ellie's place on the board was cemented even firmer.

Even though Mercedes was fighting their own battles with the FBI in this country and in Germany the Landespolizei (State Police) in downtown Berlin, they found the time to continue their battle with Franklin Industries as well, only these days it was above board and legal.

Mercedes tried to sue Franklin for not delivering a product contracted for, but a US judge threw the suit out because there was a clause in the contract that gave Franklin the right to void the signed contract if it was determined that the signee had tried to defraud Franklin Industries. This was evidenced by what was showing up daily in the news and apparently the judge had watched the daily news reports along with the rest of the country.

Next up, they tried to say that corporate pirates employed by Franklin had stolen the plans for this revolutionary new unit from Mercedes in the first place. They produced evidence that they had been working on that very thing for twenty years, but when a comparison of the two units was made they were not alike, not in any way, shape, or form so that fizzled out too.

The corporate offices in Berlin had even gone out and bought a vehicle with one of these new units in it, then commenced to take it apart to see what made it tick. But the main problem with that idea was that as soon as the computers case was opened in order to get to the operating program, an automatic internal virus wiped the program clean and the unit's usefulness was destroyed forever. Even the Chinese and Japanese had tried to do this with the same results and they ended up with a vehicle without a working operating computer unit. The only way to fix it was to buy a new unit and have it installed, tho this cost them another four thousand plus dollars.

With all this going on, it didn't come as a surprise they began to receive notices that the units that were coming off the line, at least for the past two weeks, were defective. The complaint was that there were parts of the operating unit that did not perform as it was supposed to. According to these complaints, a portion of the units, not all of them, would not recognize traffic signs or acknowledge traffic lights. Everyone, from Nash down to the line foreman, was hard pressed to understand why, but when they disassembled a defective unit, they found that a key component had not been connected to an activator. The computer was doing its job, but when it tried to make the unit respond to its commands, it couldn't or wouldn't work, either way it was something they had to fix and right away.

Each of the units that came off the line had a serial number stamped on it and there was a barcode right under it. As the unit progressed down the line, the barcode was scanned at various places and a record of when it passed particular point in the line was produced. By using these records, the problem was traced down to a single employee, her name was Polly Straus. None of the units functioned that passed her station while she was working.

Instead of firing her straight away, she was turned over to Regina and after that woman got done with Polly, she was arrested, then officially fired when she went to jail for industrial sabotage. However, she never went to trial, she skipped bail and flew off to Germany where she promptly disappeared. They couldn't prove it, but they were sure that Mercedes had something to do with that too.

With things running smoothly once more at Franklin and with Nash's jaw completely healed, he asked Ellie to go with him to Aitutaki. "Where or what in the hell is Aitutaki? I never heard of it," she asked, rolling over and into his arms.

"It's a small island in the South Pacific, the Cook Islands to be exact and it's owned by New Zealand so they speak English there. At this exclusive Pacific Resort we could rent a bungalow that's right on the beach and we could have all our meals catered if we wanted or we could go to one of the many excellent restaurants on the island, two of which are right there at this resort."

"It sounds wonderful. How long to you plan on keeping me there?" she asked, snuggling deeper into his embrace.

"As long as I can. I think a week should do it, although we can stay longer if we want, which I do."

"And what sort of devilment you have up that devious sleeve of yours?"

"To plan get you naked and keep you like that for a week. Really though, think about it. We've been putting in some exceptionally long hours these past few months and I thought that it'd be a good idea to get away for a while. With the production lines running smoothly once more and the development of my next project coming off the drawing board, and moving into preliminary assembly, they don't need either of us for a while. Shit, the money is rolling in so fast that the finance department is hard pressed to keep up with it and you know it. Say yes and let's get out of town for a while. If you do, we can leave all this cold weather, the snow and the slush behind. If you don't want to go down there, then you name a place and I'll make it happen."

"No, that resort sounds like heaven. When do you want to make this happen?" she asked, nestling against him even tighter and throwing one of her legs over his tight stomach.

"I made a few calls earlier and they told me that they can accommodate us Tuesday, starting at noon. I also checked with the airlines and from LA, we take New Zealand Air to Rarotonga. From there we move over to Air Rarotonga and they will fly us to the island. The total flying time is going to be twenty or so hours, that's from the time we leave Detroit until we land on Aitutaki. We will be in the air for seventeen of those hours."

"Alright Mr. Travel Agent, make it happen, but I expect you to work your ass off this coming Monday."

"Alright, but I need you to do me a favor before we board that jet. I want you to leave your bosses hat here when we board that

that first flight. I don't want to hear about Franklin Industries from the time we get to Metro till we get back there. Deal? All I want to do is enjoy a beautiful woman and her charms, bask in the light of her wit and be smothered with her warmth, and we damn sure don't need a CEO or the company problems to come with us."

She crawled up to his face, kissed him, complete with tongue and all, then grasp that growing staff between his legs and said, "I will do all that just so long as you bring this with you."

"You can bet on that happening, lady. In Spades."

Chapter Nineteen

The flight was a long one, but traveling in first class helped alleviate most of the perceived hardship. They were able to sleep a lot by using their seats ability to convert into a bed of sorts and they played cards, chess and used their notebooks to read books while awake. Consequently, they were well rested when the aircraft landed on the island at two in the afternoon. They were met by the islands staff and escorted to the main building of the resort where they checked in and were then taken to their bungalow.

"Oh--my--God!" Ellie exclaimed when she walked through the front door of the cabin. She could see through the building, out the patio door, all the way to the beach and the view was spectacular to say the least. While Nash gave the two bellhops a tip, Ellie kicked her shoes off, sat on the edge of the bed and pulled her nylons off, they landed on the shoes. Then she was out the door and heading straight for the white sands of the beach. As soon as the bellhops were gone, Nash grabbed a couple of towels and followed his beautiful traveling partner out the patio door. His shoes made it all the way to the sunken hot tub, that's where he left them and he too had his bare feet in the sand.

Before he could get to Ellie, she sat down on the sand, although she never took her eyes off the turquoise waters of the lagoon.

The waves that reached this beach was about two to four inches high, they were not like the four to five foot rollers that were crashing against the coral reef about two hundred yards out. He sat down next to her and when he did, she turned to him and said, "We're moving here and never leaving this island. My God, this is stunningly beautiful, I never knew places the likes of this existed. I'm sure glad that we didn't bring all the clothing that I had laid out, all I'm going to need is my swimming suit."

"Think about this, lady, here swimming suits are optional," he said unbuttoning his shirt.

She looked at him, stood up and pulled her clothes off, but left her panties on and then ran into the water. As soon as it was deep enough, she dove in headfirst, the water was about mid-thigh and she was thoroughly happy for the first time since his beating and her rape. Coming here had been a good idea, a really good idea for the both of them.

~♥~

During the next five days they got dressed only once to leave their love nest and to be around other people. They went up to the main lodge for a late supper and then went into the lounge to do some dancing and down a few drinks, although they seldom took their eyes off one another and were touching constantly. It was while they were seated off to the right of the bandstand and the band was taking a break that Nash got up, pulled a small round box from his pants pocket and got down on one knee. Even though Ellie thought she knew what was coming next she was already crying happy tears, she couldn't help it.

"Miss Ellie Masterson will you marry me?" he asked looking deeply into her already wet, but happy eyes.

In front of a crowd of about twenty or so people, she flung her arms around his neck and threw herself on him, whereas they both toppled over onto the dance floor locked in an embrace.

When their lips separated, she said loudly enough to be heard across the dance floor, "YES, oh God, yes." The other patrons and staff applauded and continued with whatever they were doing.

Later that night, much later in fact, she lay in the moonlight that was flooding the room and held her hand up so she could look at the ring he'd put on her finger, the third finger of her left hand and was amazed that this had finally happened to her. For years she thought and believed that all she wanted was a career, but tonight had proved her wrong. The love that she felt inside her body boiled and churned within her and threatened to burst out and drown them. Nash had done to her what no man had ever done, he'd accepted her as she was, unequivocally. She felt like a woman was born to feel. He'd somehow tamed her unbridled sexuality, ignored her outburst of frustration, which at times could be fierce, overlooked that mean streak in her and even seemed to enjoy her quirkiness.

She did things like make sure everything in her closet was arranged according to usage and color, her dresser drawers were the same way. When she washed her hair, she would always brush it dry; she hated using a hair dryer. As Nash found out, when she truly climaxed, her legs would quiver to such an extent that at first he though she was having an epileptic fit. There were other things that were uniquely Ellie and they were what made her special to him. He'd overlooked all those things and placed a ring on her finger, and for that she would be eternally grateful.

She turned to look at the sleeping man lying next to her. She watched the rise and fall of his chest and the gentle flaring of his nostrils as he breathed. Without waking him, she placed her hand over his genitals and said, "This is mine, now and forever." Then she took his hand and put it on her pubis and said, "And this is yours, exclusively, now and forever." And she meant every word of those statements.

~♥~

They spent three more days alone in their bungalow before leaving to make that long trip back to civilization and all of the problems that went with it. Several times during the trip, Ellie held her hand next to the window to stare at her ring, then sometimes she'd turn and kiss her man, causing him to look at her and wonder what was going on in that lovely head of hers. Yes, she had a man, a man that made her extremely happy.

December was in full swing when they landed in Michigan, there was a light dusting of snow on the ground and the temperature was only nineteen degrees. They ended up having to run from the terminal to the limo because their jackets and coat were packed away, neither of them had even thought about the weather being this cold when they left that island paradise. Jerome was standing there with the car door open for them and it looked as though he was happy to see them, judging by the size of his smile.

As Jerome eased the limo onto Interstate 94 West, Ellie asked, "Okay, so what's been going on. You look like the cat that swallowed the canary." Since it was Saturday, she figured it had something to do with football; she was not prepared for what he said next.

"Gina has a fella. I guess he's alright as far is guy's go, but there's something about him that I don't trust or like, so I stay away when he's visiting."

"So talk to me, Mr. Newsman. How'd she meet him? Did she finally go out on a date?" Gina was not an overly beautiful woman on the outside, in fact she was a plain Jane, but she was terrific on the inside and loved by everyone who knew her. She was about forty-five years old and had two children, two boys that seldom, if ever, contacted their mother. They had no idea what sort of special woman she was and that was their loss, but

Ellie absolutely loved her and treated her more like her sister. To make things even better, she and Nash got along fabulously so it was a win, win, in Ellie's book.

"He came to the house when they delivered the new washer and dryer you ordered before you left on vacation. He and Gina talked for a long time afterwards and that night they went out to dinner together. He's been by the house every other night since then."

"Has he spent the night there yet?" Nash asked, red flags were going off in his head over this latest revelation.

"No, I don't think so, but he normally stays for a few hours after their dates. I don't think their sleeping together, but I don't know that for sure."

"Jerome, Miss Ellie and I are going to talk for a while, please excuse us." He then closed the partition between the front and rear of the vehicle. Ellie sat there looking questioningly at him, until he said, "I smell a rat here. I think we should take a closer look at this fellow, especially after all that's happened since we started this project. Then, if it's nothing I'll be the first to congratulate Gina."

Ellie pulled her cell phone from her purse and called Mike Masters, but he had nothing of interest to relay to her. Her next call went to Regina and she didn't know anything about this man or Gina dating him. "Regina, I trust Gina, but Jerome doesn't think much of this guy and I have to pay attention to his qualms. Would you look into this for me?"

"Absolutely, we'll get right on it."

Turning to Nash, Ellie said, "Damn, I hope this guys on the up and up for Gina's sake. She deserves to be happy for a change." She reached for the partition and opened it so she could talk to Jerome. "So, how's our boys in maze and blue doing?"

While they talked about football, Nash sat there thinking about a stranger being in the house. And when did Ellie buy a new washer and drier? He turned to Ellie and asked, "When did you buy this washer and drier?"

"I didn't, I thought you did?" she replied, then looked at Jerome but he didn't have anything to say about that.

Without a second's hesitation, he said, "Jerome, take us to the Embassy Hotel downtown, it's on Huron Street. We'll be staying there tonight."

"What do you think is going on?" Ellie asked, suddenly concerned.

"I'm not sure, but until Regina's people check out the house, we're not going anywhere near it." He reached for his cell and dialed her number. Five minutes later Regina and three of her men were headed for Ellie's home.

Meanwhile, Ellie got on her cell and had Gina pack an overnight bag for her and then asked her to leave the house too. "Come to the Embassy Hotel on Huron, we'll have a room for you when you get there."

"What's the matter? Are you alright?" Gina asked.

"No, I mean yes, I'm fine. Just do as I asked and I'll explain when I see you."

She ended the call and put the phone in her purse. "You don't think Mercedes is at it again, do you?" she asked looking at Nash.

"Like I said, I'm not sure. It's just a gut feeling and I hope I'm wrong, but why take the chance. Let's wait until Regina works her magic and see what she turns up."

At the hotel, Ellie rented an executive suite for herself and Nash and a two-bedroom suite for Gina and Jerome, in fact their suite was right next to hers and Nash's. Jerome had just finished putting the traveler's luggage in their suite when Gina showed up looking confused.

Instead of questioning Gina in front of the men, the two women went down to the lounge, ordered drinks and Ellie waited until the drinks were on the table before starting.

"Jerome tells me you have a fellow that's interested in you."

"Yes, his name is Matt, that's short for Mathew. His last name is Jones. I met him when he delivered the washer and drier you ordered before you went on vacation."

Ignoring the appliances for now, Ellie asked, "How many dates have you had with him?"

"Five. Usually he comes to the house and picks me up, then we go out and after the date is over, I invite him in, not for sex, but for a late-night snack and some stimulating conversation. He's really nice and I think you'd like him. He was supposed to come over tonight, but he called about two hours ago and said he had to work late and wouldn't be able to make it."

"So, you haven't had sex with him so far, right?"

"No, that's not what I said. I said he didn't come to the house for sex. I have been to his apartment twice and we enjoyed ourselves there, but never at your place. What's this all about anyway? Am I not allowed to have a man in my life?"

"Gina, you're a big girl and can do anything you want. But think about this, neither me or Nash ordered any appliances, that's because there was nothing wrong with the washer and drier that was in the house already. I don't know if you're aware of the all problems we've had getting this new product that Franklin Industries has developed into production, but part of it has to do with Nash getting beat-up and my problem as well. Since then, there has been a certain amount of corporate espionage taking place, numerous courtroom battles and even sabotage at the plant. So you see, when this man or men delivered those appliances unexpectedly, it should have raised red flags all over the place.

But then that's my fault for not keeping you informed about what was going on, not yours."

"And you think that my Matt is a part of this?" she asked looking crestfallen.

"Yes, we do. And until Regina checks out those appliances and the rest of the house, we are staying here."

While the two women were in the elevator going back up to their suite's, Ellie called Regina. "I just talked with Gina and the name of this man is Mathew, or Matt Jones. You might even be able to lift a few fingerprints off those appliances if we're lucky." Then she looked at Gina and asked, "You haven't used them yet, have you?"

"No, and neither has Jerome. I'd have known if he did, he always leaves mess when he uses the soap and other things in that room."

Regina said, "I heard. Okay, we are just now rolling up to your place. I'll call you as soon as we know anything, definite."

Regina got out of the passenger side of the van and punched in the code for the front gate, then got back into the vehicle. She directed the driver to the side door, the one that led to the dethatched three car garage, this was where Nash had moved the Packard and where other toys like the matching ATV's, snowmobiles, two huge lawnmowers, a garden tractor, stuff like that resided.

There was a coded keypad on the wall next to the door that led to the house and this time Regina had to use a list that she pulled from a man's style wallet she kept in her back pocket. Once inside, she stopped the three men she'd brought with her and said, "This is a friend's home, so don't destroy it. Dave, the washer and drier is yours, but be damn carful with them, they may be boobytrapped. Carl, you take the staff quarters. Joe, you've got the basement. I'll take the owners bedrooms and we'll all get together to tackle this main level. Let's go and like I said, be careful."

When Dave opened the door to the laundry room, he stood off to one side and let it swing open on its own accord, but nothing happened. Rather than go charging in there, he looked to see if there were any inferred beams, there were none. Emboldened, he entered and pulled out his ever-present flashlight, and the first thing he did was look behind both appliances. He checked them twice, although everything looked to be normal, there were no extra wires or red flags there. Before opening the doors to either appliance, he pulled the electrical plugs to the machines and laid them on the tops of them. He then turned the gas valve off that went to the drier; this was a gas drier, a really nice one too.

While he was doing this, Regina let herself into Ellie's bedroom and the first place she looked was the closet, it was the size of most people's bedroom. When she got inside the closet she could smell something amiss there, but couldn't put her finger on it. It just didn't smell right and knowing Ellie like she did, she'd never have allowed her closet to smell like this. She attributed the smell to being closed up for the past week and a half and left it at that. After she backed out of the closet, she took another look around the suite, then left.

Then suddenly she knew what that smell was.

Standing in the hall she shouted as loud as she could, "Everyone, get back on the bus. NOW! This place is not safe."

When she got to the door that they'd entered the house from, she smelled that odor again only this time her nose detected the smell of rotten eggs, that was a sign of gas in her book. "Let's go, we don't have a moment to lose," she demanded.

They had just gotten the van started when the entire house exploded and the force of the blast was strong enough that it blew the van sideways and into the garage, it was ten feet away. The van and the wall of the garage that faced the house was forced halfway through the building before all of it came to a stop just short of Nash's beloved Packard.

The explosion caused several fires to break out in the debris, but there wasn't enough left of the house to continue burning for long so the fires quickly went out on their own. A lot of the house had fallen into the basement, but there were no fires there. The garage that was attached to the house was damaged too, but at least it was still standing, well partially anyway.

In the other garage, the van that Regina and her people were in lay on its side, its windows on the driver's side were blown out. One of the men, Joe, moved and tried to turn his head but Dave was laying on him. Struggling with the dead weight, he got one of his arms free and rolled the man off him, then sort of sat up on what used to be the right side of the van. Looking towards the front seat he saw the van driver, he was hanging from his seatbelt and dripping blood down onto Regina. She was still in the passenger seat, although she was either unconscious or dead, he didn't know which. He looked at Dave and knew he was dead, one side of his head was stove in and his unseeing eyes were bulging out of his skull.

Instead of saving himself and ignoring the others, he managed to make his way to the front of the van and get Regina's seatbelt undone. Rather than trying to get her out of the driver's door, he kicked the rest of the windshield out. Once he was out of the van, he pulled Regina free and moved her to a section of the garage that was more stable and untouched. With her safe and resting comfortably on a rubber mat next to the Packard, he pulled a cell phone from his pocket and made the call to 911.

~♥~

Nash and Ellie were just leaving their suite; they were on their way to get a bite to eat when her cell phone rang. "Hello," she responded after looking at the caller ID, but all it said was 'Cell Phone, MI'.

"Is this Miss Ellie Masterson, CEO of Franklin Industries?" the caller asked.

"Yes, it is. Who is this?"

"I'm Detective Sergeant Yancy Goldsmith and I'm with the Michigan State Patrols bomb squad. There was a massive explosion this afternoon and it involved your house. I got your number from Ms. Regina Williams, she asked me to call you. I'm here at the hospital with Ms. Williams, she has been admitted to the hospital. I was wondering if you could come to the University of Michigan's Medical Center to see her and while you're here maybe you could answer a few of my questions."

"We'll be there in fifteen minutes." Ellie turned to Nash and said, "Get Jerome up, we're going to the hospital. Regina is there and she's been injured."

"What happened?" he asked, then began walking down the hall towards Gina and Jerome's suite.

"I don't know. Just get him moving and tell him to bring the car around to the front. Tell him we'll be there in five minutes and let him know we're going to the U of M Medical Center."

Ellie went back into the suite to change out of the dress she had on and quickly got into a pair of jeans and a blouse, then she swapped her high heeled shoes for a pair of white walking shoes. Meanwhile, Nash stood there watching her and was growing impatient, he wanted to get moving. Regina was a good friend of his and he wanted to go to her as rapidly as he could.

Jerome dropped them off at the front door of the hospital and Nash was hard pressed to keep up with Ellie as she walked ahead of him. On their way to the hospital she'd called ahead and knew what room they had Regina in, so they didn't stop at the reception desk. When they entered the room, Regina was propped up in bed and talking with a man they'd never see before.

"Take it easy you two or you'll pop a cork. I'm fine, just a bump on my hard damn head, that's all. They said they were going to keep me overnight, but I nixed that idea right off. Anyway, this is Detective Goldsmith, but he answers to the name of Yancy. I've known him for years, we're old friends so be honest with him. He'd like to talk to you later, but I've already clued him in on everything pertinent to this case so he's leaving for now."

"So, what the hell happened? And do I have a home to return to?"

"The house is a complete write off. Two of my team was killed in the explosion that destroyed your house. My van, with the four of us in it, was blasted into next week, only Joe and me survived that ride. I will tell you this, right there at the last while we were still in the house, I thought I detected the rotten-egg smell of gas, but apparently it was already too late for us by then. Anyway, I have to undergo two more tests for the doctors and then they're going to let me go. If you don't mind sticking around and waiting, I'm going to need a ride home."

"So, how's Joe doing, is he here too?" Nash asked.

"Nope, he only had a few cuts and bruises so they treated and released him. He took a cab and went home about fifteen minutes ago."

Just then a nurse came in, loaded Regina onto a wheelchair and whisked her off to complete her tests. As soon as they were gone, Ellie sat down and looked out the window to wait while Nash headed off to find Jerome and the limo. He could have saved himself the effort though, Jerome was parked less than thirty feet from the front door. The limo was running and he was out of the main stream of traffic. And it was apparent that he wasn't budging from that spot until his boss came out.

Nash got into the front passenger seat and took a closer look at Jerome's face, then asked, "Seriously, what was it that you didn't like about this guy Gina was dating?"

"When I met him, he couldn't hold eye contact with me and I got the impression that he was always looking for something. That first night that he came to the house, he asked Gina for a tour and that in itself wasn't strange, but the only places he wanted to see was the basement, the downstairs closets and the pantry, that was the room that was the closest to the laundry room. Then he was asking questions like how often do we do laundry and if there is anything else stored in the laundry room. Now I ask you, what sort of man goes around asking questions about a laundry room? The guy gave me the creeps."

"What'd he look like?" Nash asked.

"He had dark brown, almost black hair and his ears sort of stuck out a little more than normal. He had a muscular build, but a bit of a paunch if you asked me. Brown eyes, somewhat of a crooked nose, thin lips, and---, oh yeah, he had a blue tattoo of an anchor on his right hand; I saw it when we shook hands. And that's another thing, he had a weak handshake. Taking hold of his hand was like grabbing a limp dishrag, if you know what I mean. It was while I was shaking his hand that I decided I didn't like the man, there was no sincerity to the handshake."

"Did you meet the guy every time he came to the house?"

"No, just that first time. That was the day after you guys left. But it's my job to keep an eye on things when Miss Ellie's not home and I take that job quite seriously, that's why I knew every time he came through the front gate, when they left, when they came home and more importantly, when he left."

"Too bad you didn't get a photo of him. I would like to see what he looks like."

"There are security cameras outside the house, but most likely all that was destroyed in the explosion----wait a minute here. There is a separate camera system at the front gate and it makes its own recordings. I know because one of my jobs is to replace the DVD once a week."

"When was the last time you changed DVD's?"

"I always do it Sunday mornings before Miss Ellie gets out of bed, but I didn't change it last Sunday, you guys weren't home and not that many people came and went."

"Where are the old DVD's kept?" Nash asked with a glimmer of hope. It was still Saturday, that meant there should be a picture of this guy on the DVD that was in the recorder.

"In the media room of the house, sorry." But like Nash, Jerome was thinking the same thing, there was still a chance that an image of this guy remained.

Before he could say anything, Nash said, "When Miss Ellie and Regina joins us, take us out to the house so we can check on that DVD."

"Can do. And if you need someone to bend this guy's head a little, I'd be glad to volunteer for that job too."

"Thanks, but I think we have that covered."

Ellie came out the hospital door first and as soon as she did Jerome moved the car over next to her. Then a nurse came out wheeling Regina in a wheelchair and suddenly Jerome saw Regina in an entirely different light. Regina was beautiful in his eyes. Maybe he'd been looking in all the wrong places for the replacement of his girlfriend, he should have been looking right under his nose. She might be a little older than he was, but what difference did a few years mean in this day in age.

~♥~

The limo with three passengers in it pulled up to the open gate and that's when Ellie and Nash got their first look at what was left of her house. While Jerome went to the locked watertight cabinet on the other side of the gate that the security gear was in, they couldn't take their eyes off of the carnage the explosion had created. Jerome opened the cabinet using a key that was on a ring of keys he carried with him and removed the disk. He turned and looked at them with a smile on his face, then he suddenly seemed to look into the air and collapse where he stood.

Nash knew that look, he'd seen it before in Iraq and this was not the time to sit there thinking about it. In an instant he dove over the front seat and as he did he shouted, "Get on the floor and stay there!" A second or two later he had the limo moving, while the two women were hanging on for dear life and getting onto the floorboards of the car. Instead of going away from the gate, he drove up the driveway towards the mess left from the explosion. As he did, two more rounds smashed through the back window and the passenger's side of the limo.

Driving over and through the wreckage, he pulled the limo behind what was left of the attached garage and got out. His destroyed Jeep was still in the garage and that was his destination this time. He wanted to get to it because he kept a 10mm Glock taped to the underside of the dashboard; it was right next to the steering wheel's shaft.

Once he was armed, he rejoined the women in the limo and asked, "Is there a back way off the property?"

"There's a locked gate on the other side of the tennis court, but I don' t think it has been used in years. In fact, there's a bush that's grown right in the middle of it," Ellie said, as she sat up on the floor and looked over the seat at him. Regina stayed put, she knew better than to move and she was already calling the police on her cell.

Nash got the car moving again and he drove through flower gardens, over small trees and bushes, down two steps and around the tennis court. While the limo did all this, several more bullet holes appeared in the windows, but this time Nash was driving from a semi prone position and barely peeking over the dash so the rounds missed him. He spotted the gate, mashed his foot onto the accelerator and they crashed through the gate going about fifty miles an hour. On the other side, he found himself on a gravel road that fed onto a paved road about a hundred feet from where they were. Moments later they were headed away from the scene at an insane speed, so Nash slowed down as the big car crossed a major road. Then he turned onto Whitmore Lake Road and headed south and when he checked his mirrors, no one was following them that he could see.

"Head for the cop shop on East Huron," Regina said getting off the floor and taking a seat once more. As she did, Ellie followed suit and both women strapped themselves in. Then she called the police again and said, "Make sure you get the DVD disk that Jerome was holding when he was shot."

When she hung up, Ellie said, "Why in the hell do they want us dead? Those units will still be produced by our replacements and anyone should be able to figure that out."

"Who would replace you if you were no longer alive?" Regina asked stopping for a red light.

"Charlie Anderson, why?"

Nash replied, "I've known Charlie for years and he's always wanted to be the boss. I like the guy but he can be a bit of a pain when it comes to his work ethics, he's very dedicated, if you know what I mean. Regina, could you ask your people to look into this for us?"

Regina called Holly and put her on it, this sort of thing was right up her alley.

At the police station, they counted no less that ten bullet holes in the limo. Regina elected to stay with her friends at the police station while the detective had a squad car take Ellie and Nash to their hotel and he assigned the two uniformed officers that took them there to stay and guard them. So, with two officers sitting outside the door to their suite, Ellie and Nash settled in, took a shower and ordered room service.

"I sure am going to miss that man," Ellie said, meaning Jerome.

After their showers and a good meal, they were seated in the lounge area of the suite when Nash's cell buzzed. He answered it when he saw it was Regina. "Well, what's up?" he asked.

They talked for a few moments before Regina smiled and said, "Okay, Sherlock, listen up. When the cops got to the house they found Jerome, only he wasn't dead. The bullet did hit him in the chest, but it just nicked his heart and exited his back, at least that's what the doctors said anyway. The doctor said he was operated on as soon as they got him to the hospital and that the operation went so well that he's in a room already."

"Oh yes, the responding officers did retrieve the DVD disk and yes, this guy's mug was on it. Detective Goldsmith has already gotten a warrant issued for this assholes arrest except Matt Jones is not his name, it's Thomas Thacker. They recognized him from a previous arrest less than two months ago. He was brought in on a murder charge, but without any hard evidence he was released two days later."

"What sort of murder charge?" he asked, looking at Ellie and smiling.

"He's a suspected contract killer and he works out of Detroit. He'd killed a union organizer named Bret Cavendish, but with no evidence to hold him, he was released."

"Thanks Buddy, I own you one on this," Nash said.

"And I'll be there to collect, you can bet the cat and your next T bone steak on that account," and she snickered over her response so he'd know what she was doing.

When he hung up, he turned to Ellie and said, "Jerome's alive. They have him in the hospital, but he's in serious condition. They've already operated on him and he's in a room."

"How bad was he?" she asked.

"The bullet nicked his heart, that's why the operation. The other good news is they retrieved the DVD and we now know the real name of Gina's boyfriend. He's a contract killer, a killer for hire and he's not a nice man, at least according to the police and Regina. They are looking for him as we speak."

"Then if he's a contract killer, that means we have to find out who hired him in the first place," she said.

Before he could respond to that statement, Ellie's phone rang, it was Regina again. "Well, it's been confirmed, Charlie Anderson's the inside man and the one who was working with Fray Bennington from the beginning. He only pretended to be helping you develop this new system, all the while he was working behind the scenes to sabotage it. He's the one who hired that woman to do what she did on the assembly line and he's the one who gave the information to those men so they could submarine those tests in Canada. Once we started looking at him instead of Bennington, it all became clear and it came together. I'm on my way home now, but the police have also issued an arrest warrant for him as well."

"So, what you're saying is that it wasn't Mercedes after all, is that right?"

"Oh sure, Mercedes had a hand in it, but not to the extent that we thought. They fought you on this development, but they did this legally and above board. Fray and Charlie was the catalyst behind all the other problems you've been having. By the way, the fire department called Detective Goldsmith while I was there and told him they had figured out what happened at your house."

"When Thacker and some other guy delivered the washer and drier to your house, he apparently fixed the gas line so that it would leak slowly and only into the walls of the house. That had to be the reason he kept going back to the house, he was making sure that the gas wasn't detectable on the inside. With the house's walls full of natural gas, all he had to do is call this disposable cell phone that he'd put in the wall when they installed the appliances and the tiny spark created when it rang was all that was needed to ignite the gas. They figured that there was enough gas in there to blow up a dozen homes like the one you had."

"So Charlie's going to be arrested on murder charges as well, right?" Ellie asked.

"That's right. Now I'm going to get some rest so I can be bright eyed and bushy tailed when they arrest them. Good night."

Ellie turned to Nash, gave him a kiss and explained what Regina had just told her.

"But they haven't arrested them yet, so we have to remain on guard. It helps to know who's after you, but in reality our situation has not changed yet. We are going to stay here until those two are safely behind bars."

"What are we going to do, sit and stare at the walls or that damn TV?"

He stood up and pulled his pants off, he was already barefoot after his shower. "I can think of several things we could do and none of them involves clothing, and this is not a spectator sport either, however you have to participate for this to work right."

"OOOOHH, I like your idea. So then two has to play this sport?" she asked undoing her robe.

"Yes, this is a sport best played by two," whereas he reached down and helped her to her feet and pulled her robe the rest of the way off her body.

Before they got started, she said, "When we finish, if I can still walk, I need to talk to Gina, then we are going to the hospital and visit a friend."

His hand slipped between her legs and he moved them apart to give him freer access to what lie between them. She complied easily to the demands his hand was making and moaned as he found what he was seeking. Locked together, from lips to their groins, they fell to the floor together.

Chapter Twenty

At noon on Monday the Lincoln Dealership there in Ann Arbor called Nash on his cell phone and told him that his new car was in. It was one that had his invention installed in it and he was anxious to get his hands on his very own toy.

When they left the dealership in his new, fully equipped Lincoln Navigator, Ellie felt special. This was not a CEO that was with him, nor was this a work-related sort of event, no she felt special because she was a woman and not just any woman, she was his woman. Any memories of the rape or of her past life were long gone, buried into her deepest memories and all she could think about was her man and how he made her feel when she was with him.

She watched as he programmed in their destination, today it was a little town near Lansing called Laingsburg. "Why on earth Laingsburg? I've never even heard of that town," she asked, watching him.

"I've been there before, many times in fact and there's an old-fashioned bikers bar there, it's called The Burg Sports Bar & Grill, it's on the main street of town. We're going there to see if anyone's around that I know. I met this bunch a few years back and contrary to most beliefs, they are not all druggies or thieves, in fact, most of them have good paying jobs and pay their taxes just like we do. True, they can be a bit rough around the edges at times, but take a close look at me, I fit right in with this bunch."

When he finished programming the cars computer, he flipped the switch on the dashboard and they felt the unit take over the vehicle. As it pulled out into traffic, without any help from them, he turned to look at Ellie; this was her first real ride in a rig that had one of these things installed in it. Although she wasn't looking at him, she was watching were the vehicle was taking them and she was all eyes. Several times, she looked over at him and it was a bit disconcerting to see him looking at her and not touching the steering wheel or even paying any attention to where they were going. Nevertheless, being the trooper that she was, it only took her about five miles to finally relax and trust the machine to get them where they were going safely.

That's because, unlike humans, the eight active sensors that were located around the vehicle fed information into the computer at the rate of thirty times a second, this allowed the vehicle to respond to any dangers much more rapidly that any human could. Another feature that was built into the autos computer was its ability to learn and interface with other computers whenever in was in close proximity to another computer, such as passing one another on the road or even stopping next to a vehicle at a stop light. In a split second an uplink would take place between the computers via the sensors and whatever traffic or road conditions, or weather information one computer had stored in it, that information would be transferred to any other computers that was within twenty feet of it. This allowed any other like computer to know what was ahead and then it could make decisions that would safely guide a vehicle through or around any dangerous situation. This was just one of the many features and innovations that made Nash's invention stand out from the others.

Of course, all this was patented. In all there were a hundred and three patens on this one unit alone and several more on the installed black box that went with it. With over five hundred thousand of these vehicles already on the road, Nash and Franklin Industries was making money faster than it could be printed. As an added bonus, older cars and trucks were being traded in at the rate of a five thousand a day, everyone wanted one of these things.

The new project Nash was working on these days was a way to retrofit the existing vehicles that were already on the road with one of these units, but the conversion was going to be expensive. The initial projections were thirty-four hundred dollars for the unit and they could only be installed at a licensed dealership by trained technicians. This way, the people who owned vintage vehicles or didn't want a new one, or couldn't afford to buy a new vehicle, they could be retrofitted with one of these new units.

But they knew it would just be a matter of time before restorers and shade tree mechanics learned how to do this install, so this contingency was also taken into account by building failsafe devices into these units to prevent them from being compromised. If a unit's central computer didn't receive certain information from the sensors, in a prescribed order and with a sufficient strength, they would not work, meaning that specialize tools and equipment were needed for the install.

Nash and Ellie discussed this on their way to Laingsburg for a while, before the conversation moved on to their up and coming wedding.

"I talked with my dad and he's going to come, but he's not giving me away. I asked my brother, Marsh, to do that and he's agreed. There's been too much said between me and my parents in the past ten years for it to all be forgiven overnight, but this wedding is going to help."

"My football buddies are going to be there, you can bet on that, and I have to warn you they can be a handful if they are not watched closely. That goes even double for this bunch we're going to see today. Thank God most of them will be bringing their wives to the wedding, that should slow them down a little, I hope."

The trip took them about an hour and twenty minutes to travel the sixty-five miles between Ann Arbor and Laingsburg, and the vehicle even parked itself near the building. He took Ellie's hand as they entered the bar and he directed her to a table. Once they had a drink in front of them, Nash asked the owner, he was sitting at the end if the bar, "Has Bobby Winfield been in today?"

"Yeah, he was in earlier. He'll be back in a few minutes, he had to go help one of his buddies get his ride started."

When he rejoined Ellie at the table they discussed the pros and cons of this bar being a meeting place as opposed to meeting at a McDonald's or Starbucks. As they were doing this, three men came in dressed in black leathers and carrying their helmets. Bobby was one of them and when he looked over at the couple seated at the table he recognized Nash. "Well suck my dick and call it a lollypop. Hi Nash, long time no see."

When he got to the table he took a seat and looked lustfully at Ellie, he liked what he saw. "Easy there, hormones, this is my future wife, Ellie. Ellie, this is Bobby so play nice with him, he's a friend."

"What the fuck brings you to this neck of the woods? You get lost?" Bobby asked, turning his attention to Nash. He'd talked this way for so many years that the word fuck wasn't considered as cussing anymore.

"Nope, we're here to see you. I came in to see if we're still as good of friends as we were a while back."

"We are, that is unless you've been buggering my old lady, then I'm going to have to castrate you. What's up?"

This was so like Bobby, he didn't beat around the bush, he got business done first, then socialized. "I suppose you've seen me on TV and read about my invention?"

"I have, in fact Missy and I own a car with one of those things in it, WOW! Although I wouldn't call it driving, it's more like riding in a car than driving. The problem is we've only had it for a little over a week and to date I have yet to drive it, she won't let me behind the wheel."

"Well, there's been some resistance at the corporate level to this invention of mine. A little while ago our house was blown up and two people were killed when it blew. We have a good idea who did it, but he's gone underground and we can't find him. His name is Thomas Thacker but I'm sure he's going by an assumed name. At any rate, the police went through his place and found zilch point shit, and no one has seen this asshole anywhere. That means he's probably still after us and I want him found."

After looking at Ellie, Nash continued. "What I'd like you to do is put the word out to your buddies around Michigan, Indiana and Ohio and see if they can turn him out. I have a photo of what the guy looks like if that will help?"

"It will. Why don't you get the photo while I dig up my computer? It's in the saddlebags of my ride, I'll be right back." He got up with Nash and the two of them went out together.

When the door closed, Ellie sat there looking at the other bikers seated at the bar and felt sort of abandoned and alone, but none of them even paid any attention to her. When Nash was with her, she felt strong and in charge of things and she was too, but that rape was never that far from her mind and it still bothered her at times like this. Nash and Bobby came back in together and retook their seats laughing about something.

Bobby opened his computer, turned it on and waited for it to sign on. While he did this, Nash and he were talking about some other guy in the gang and what happened during a rodeo, (a long ride with the entire gang), they went on this past summer. He took the photo from Nash and looked at it, then sat there for a moment or two and closed his computer, shutting it off.

Nash looked at him inquisitively, so Bobby said, "Hang loose there buddy. I already know exactly where this fucking ass-wipe's at. About ten of us were in Clare doing some shopping at Jay's Sporting Goods less than a week ago when this prick comes rolling in and runs over Nell's ride, I mean he actually ran over it with that fucking 4x4 of his. He thought it was funny so instead of stopping and maybe apologizing, he drove to another part of the parking lot, gets out and goes into the store like nothing's wrong. We knew it was him that ran over the bike because Ralph heard the noise, turned and watched this asshole do it. Ralph came in and told us about it so we were waiting for him when he came out of the store about fifteen minutes later. To make a long story short, when we approached him this stupid dickhead pulled a pistol out so we took him down, tied him up and tossed him in the back of his fucking rig. Then we loaded Nell's wrecked bike in the back of his truck and we brought the entire mess down here. We changed the VIN on the truck, took some of the crap off that he'd installed on it, put a little paint on it here and there and sold it to a farmer named Rucker over near the Sleepy Hollow State Park. The farmer gave us enough to fix Nell's ride, so we're cool on that account, but that prick won't be bothering anyone else anytime soon."

"So now you've got our curiosity up. What'd you do with him?" Nash asked. Ellie sat there and was a little confused; she wasn't used to being around people like this.

"Maybe I shouldn't say too much more, I don't want to get any of the boys in trouble," he said after looking at the expression on Ellie's face.

"Listen, if you did what I think you did, then we'll probably give you a reward. In truth, Ellie and I want this asshole deader than dead and that's the bottom line here. I've got a feeling that if the cops get their hands on him first he might stand a chance of getting off Scott free, or only serving a light sentence. He needs to pay for destroying our house and killing several of our friends. Believe me, whatever you tell us will go no further, you have my word on that, isn't that right honey?"

She looked directly at Bobby and said, "You've got my word on this."

He got up and put some money in the jukebox and soon the sounds of Taylor Swift filled the bar. When he sat back down, he looked at Ellie first, studied her face once more, then turned to Nash and said, "He's dead and maybe we should leave it at that."

"No Bobby, that won't do. We need the particulars; we need to know how this fucking prick died and just how dead he is."

"Let's go outside, I want to show you my ride," he said standing up and picking up his computer.

The three of them left the bar together and the first thing they noticed was that the weather was turning ugly, at least for Nash and Ellie it was. A light snow was falling, but a west wind was blowing it away as fast as it fell. Ellie pulled her coat around her while the two men stood next to Bobby's beautiful, fully decked out Harley Hog. Bobby motioned for Ellie to come closer and when she did, he said, "We took that fucking idiot out in a field, stripped him down and then used him as a ramp to pull Nell's busted ride out of his rig. After that we used him as a launch point to jump our bikes over some tires. When he got so bloody that we didn't want to get anymore of his fucking shit on out rides, we set fire to him. While he burnt, for about an hour, Carl went up and got his tractor out, hooked-up a disk to it and we turned this fucker into little bitty chunks that the crows and other little wild critters seemed to like. When they got done munching on him, we used the disk again and rolled it over him until there was nothing left, not even a memory. Nowadays we don't even talk about him and never will."

"Christ, buddy, that's sort of final. Well, all I can say to that is thank you and for the service you did for us, I want you and your boys to accept our deepest gratitude and let us give you a couple hundred grand for your good deed. Use it to upgrade those bikes, or to go on a rodeo somewhere. Thanks."

Ellie stepped closer to Bobby, kissed his cheek and said, "If any you boys need a job, come and see either Nash or me and you've got one. Thank you from the bottom of my heart."

Together, they walked over to Nash's Navigator and while Ellie was getting in out of the wind, Bobby asked, "Is this one that has your invention in it?"

"It is. Would you like to go for a ride?"

"Fucken A. Let's go," and he got in the back seat looking all the world like a kid getting his first ride on a rollercoaster. He smiled at Ellie as Nash got in, but he never took his eyes off the dashboard of the massive vehicle.

As the vehicle began to move, Nash took Ellie's hand and she pulled his hand to her mouth and kissed it. It could be read in both of their eyes, it was finally over and they could begin to live again. This nightmare truly was at an end.

The End

Printed in Germany
by Amazon Distribution
GmbH, Leipzig